MISCHIEF, MAYHEM AND SHAKESPEARE

E. G. STONE

For my own furry companions:
Leah, Sammy and Minnie

PET SITTING

Hey, Cal...It's me. Neja. Look, I know things were weird the last time we saw each other but...you know how things are. Look, I'm on a job in the mortal realms and I think I found something. About your soul. I think it's important, Cal. I won't be back in Elsewhere for three days, so maybe we can just meet up then? Just...give me a call, okay? Great. Um. Bye.

-BEEP-

I listened to the message three times, my head pressed against the door to my apartment, phone to my ear. Those words, they taunted me. Tantalised me. "About your soul," she had said. Could it really be that simple? That after all this time and the tragedy that followed me, that someone had finally found my soul?

My name is Cal Thorpe and I work for Death. I used to be his marketing and public relations manager, happily working away with my rock troll assistant Yolanda and my aurai marketing associate, Agravane.

That is, when I wasn't doing other work, like solving murders or performing relationship counselling or acting as his proxy. Or losing my soul.

Somewhere between the time I lost my soul and now, I had also started to turn into what Death called a Reaper. It was almost like being Death, except I could only release someone's soul, not lead them on to wherever they were meant to go. I wasn't all-powerful, like Death. I couldn't even command a modicum of gravitas. I was just a collector of souls. A killer. Let's just say that I wasn't particularly thrilled about that revelation; in fact, I was so thrilled that I had run—I hate running —from Death's lands to Life's mansion and accepted her ridiculous devil's bargain to stabilise my condition.

So, yeah. I work for Life part-time, now, too.

I didn't really know if my foolish agreement with Life has really stabilised my condition. I did know that I could feel her power pulling at me, warring with Death's power that pulled me in a different direction. It was uncomfortable and it was annoying and it was like being the rope in a game of tug of war where each side has equal pull. I was stuck in the middle.

And you know what? Maybe that was a good thing. Maybe it *had* helped, being stuck between Life and Death. My emotional situation no longer fluctuated between hyperrational Vulcan and five year old on a sugar high. What I *did* feel was muted, dull, like there was a mediator between me and my emotions, telling me what to feel but not how to feel it.

Like just then, standing at the door and unable to

move forwards or back. Done with work for the day, I had headed up to my apartment to eat some pizza and collapse on my couch in exhaustion. Not necessarily in that order, mind you. I knew I was beyond tired. My hands were doing that funny thing where they couldn't quite grab onto things like you would expect, and I was fairly certain that my eyes weren't that blurry normally, even when wearing my glasses. But I didn't really *feel* the exhaustion, not the way you would expect.

Think of it like commenting on the weather. It's something you notice pretty much all the time, and occasionally you talk about it with someone to pass the time, but rarely do you get super worked up over it, unless there's a massive storm about to kill you. That was what my current situation was like.

Or had been like, up until the point where I got a voicemail from the djinn Neja, telling me that she might have information *about my soul*.

Neja and I had a complicated relationship. We had first met while I was toting around Al Capone's soul as a temporary patch on my condition. I had felt relatively normal, albeit with a crazy person whispering in my ear, and Neja and I had gotten on fairly well, even considering she'd worked with someone who summoned her to kill me. (It's a long story.) We both felt like whatever it was we had might be going some-where, so we made the general overtures to going on a date. Then, Neja found out I was carting a temporary soul and that my emotions weren't always my own. We had proceeded to rekill Al Capone (again, a long story) and eventually went on that date.

Sort of.

I had been emotionally unstable at the time, able to only feel anything at all for a very small number of things, none of which was Neja. She had left and that had been that. Until now.

"Oh, good, you're here."

I shoved my phone into my pocket and straightened, turning to face the owner of the deep and slightly-terrifying-yet-soothing voice: Death, and my boss. He was dressed rather casually for him, which meant that instead of a three-piece suit, matching pocket square and some sort of neck ornamentation, he was simply wearing slacks and a shirt, though these were of a quality that would have astounded most tailors. Of course, considering that his skin was black-hole dark and had shadows writhing about him as a sign of his power, the casual look didn't convey quite the same impression as it would on anyone else. Such was the situation when you worked for a Force of the Universe.

"Hello," I said, unsure of what emotion spilled over into my words. Judging by the confused look on Death's face, I gather he wasn't sure, either. "Want to come in? I've got coffee."

I unlocked the door, hardly waiting for an answer. I hadn't spoken to him for two weeks. The last time had been in his office, right after going through withdrawal from collecting souls during my brief stint as his proxy, and then being told that I was turning into a Reaper. I had run to Life directly afterwards; thankfully, I hadn't heard from her, either.

"Yes, thank you," Death said, voice formal. "I heard you managed to acquire a lifetime supply in exchange for marketing services."

"There was a stand at the Goblin Market," I said. "I talked with the owner. It's really good coffee."

We stepped into my flat and I closed the door behind us, waiting for Death to say something else. Even with my interest in coffee—oddly, this was one thing that didn't feel muted—there wasn't a whole lot to fill the void of silence that lay between us. Death wandered over to my couch and, looking at me for permission, sat. I sat in the club chair perpendicular to him.

"I also hear," Death started, his empty eyes looking down at his hands, "that you have made an agreement with my wife."

"I'm her gofer in exchange for stabilising my condition," I said. There was no use in hiding it. Death was, well, Death. I'm sure he could sense the fact that I had made that agreement the moment it had happened. I had been waiting for this confrontation for two weeks, wondering just what his reaction would be. I never expected to be reamed for it, but I did imagine he wouldn't be terribly happy. Life and Death didn't get along terribly well, as I'm sure you can imagine.

I closed my eyes and sighed. "Look, it's not that I don't like working for you. I do. A lot. But..."

"You do not wish to be a Reaper," Death said. He was acting rather calmly about the whole situation. Maybe it was just me that felt like the undercurrents in the room were getting stronger. After all, it was a cloudy day and it did look like rain. One had to be prepared. Take an umbrella.

"I don't mind collecting souls," I said. True, though the high that came with it was terrifying and addicting. I would have to get some sort of control over that sensation if I ever did become a full Reaper. "But I don't want to..."

"Kill people?" Death tilted his head slightly, now watching me intently. "I'm not surprised. You were rather squeamish when I told you what had happened."

I nodded, this time my turn to lower my gaze. While acting as Death's proxy, I had been tasked with collecting souls of the dead. I had, inadvertently, collected people's souls in the very moment before their deaths, actually killing them. It hadn't mattered to me that they were dying and would imminently be dead. I was the one responsible for taking their lives. I hadn't known. And now that I did, I wished I didn't.

"Being a Reaper isn't all about killing, Cal," Death said, giving a shrug of his hands, the shadows darting between his fingers as he moved. "It is about being present when people are faced with the possibility of dying, and offering them a way forwards. It is about maintaining the balance between Life and myself. It is about—"

"Look, it's not that I'm not grateful," I said, though it was clear as sunshine that I wasn't, "but I wasn't even *asked*."

Now, Death just looked at me with a small smile, the one you give pitiful creatures. "For that, I am sorry. But it is not my doing. Not intentionally, at least. Some part of your being began to change when you started interacting with the denizens of Elsewhere. It could even be your proximity to Elsewhere itself that is causing this continuing change. It is something that would have happened because of your birth, your blood, your history. Inevitable."

I snorted. "Great. I've got some giant cosmic hereditary disease. Why weren't any of my family Reapers, then?"

"Proximity to Elsewhere, as I said. Some beings are more drawn to the metaphysical side of things. When I released your...the loss of your soul only exacerbated the issue, accelerating it and making it an inevitability rather than a path you could choose. I am sorry for that. For starting the process that will turn you something other than human, and forcing this on you." Death did look a little contrite, but he was a hyperpowerful being. I'm sure he could lie to his not-quite-human marketing expert. I doubt it would even be all that difficult for him.

I slouched into the club chair, that niggling sensation of exhaustion growing louder, a storm on the horizon. "It's not going to stop, just because I'm working for Life, now, too. Is it?"

Death pressed his mouth into a straight line. Then, he smiled, and not from happiness, either. "I'm sorry, Cal, but you may have stabilised your emotional state by your agreement with my wife, but you have only confirmed the transformation. Even, perhaps, made it happen all the quicker. Reapers are balancers. They stand on the razor's edge between Life and myself. I utilise them more than she simply because she does not wish to give up any of her power to me, even if it is necessary. It's not...it's not just about killing people, if that makes you feel better. It's quite a bit more complicated."

"I'm sure it is," I sighed, tilting my head back. "Everything about this place is quite a bit more complicated than it should be. I just wanted to do marketing. Was that too much to ask?"

"Then you should have specified that in your contract," Death said. I lifted my head long enough to glare at him, noted that he was wearing a teasing smile, and then lowered my head again.

"If that's all, I'm a bit tired," I said. Maybe he would get the hint and leave me in peace. We could have a discussion on all the complexities of the universe another day. When I wasn't tired. And maybe pissed off. (Though, I couldn't really tell.)

"Actually, though I wanted to talk with you, I came here for another reason. I have a request." Death waited until I was sitting up slightly straighter in my chair, actually looking at him, before he continued. "I have been sent a notice requiring my presence for jury duty and—"

"Jury duty?!" I could feel my jaw drop. Even muffled, my astonishment shone through loud and clear. "You can't be serious. How would *you* possibly even—"

Death scowled, his brows drawing together and the voids that were his eyes swirling with some strong emotion. "I lost a bet."

I blinked. "Right."

"With Life."

"Okay."

Death was the one to slouch backwards and lean against the couch. "It was a long time ago, when they were just setting up the system in the colonies and Life and I made a bet. I lost. Therefore, I have to serve jury duty once every decade."

"The...colonies," I said. "As in the British colonies? As in, what, America?"

Death nodded.

I closed my eyes. "Okay." My voice had gone a little hoarse. "So, what, you want me to be your proxy again?"

"Unfortunately, no. I cannot engage a proxy for such matters. No, I need you to watch my dogs and my cat."

I opened my eyes again. Barely managed to refrain from dropping my jaw even farther. Blinked. Then, "What?"

"I kennelled them while I was on holiday because I

didn't want to add to your troubles while you were acting as my proxy. But this should just be a short duration. Two, three days at most. And I really don't want to go through the bother of kennelling them again; they always come back so out of sorts." Death brushed his knee absently with a hand, as if sweeping away some dust. Or animal fur.

"No, it's more the fact that you actually have dogs and a cat. Pets." I hadn't had a pet myself since I was a kid, and even then the dog had really belonged to the neighbours. My parents seemed to get confused every time I brought the matter up, so eventually I stopped pestering them.

I was having a hard time imagining Death with pets, unless they were monstrous, slavering creatures who would do their best to take your head off as a greeting mechanism. It was one of those thoughts that flashed across my mind like lightning, and once there, the afterimage was hard to dismiss.

Death shrugged. "They make things so much better."

I nodded. My voice was squeaky when I spoke again. "Um, so, what do I need to do?"

Death pulled out a piece of paper from his trousers pocket and handed it to me. I unfolded it and saw, scrawled in his neat handwriting, general instructions for feeding, watering, and exercising two dogs and a cat.

"Mischief and Mayhem—the dogs came with the names and won't answer to anything else, I'm afraid—

are Belgian Tervuren mixed with Fae dogs. They're quite intelligent, and very well meaning, but perhaps a bit too energetic. I suggest you use the ball chucker when playing with them." Death mimed throwing a ball and I made a mental note to google that particular device. "And Shakespeare is a purebred grimalkin. Fae cat. He was a gift from the Winter Court some centuries ago at the solstice. No matter what he says, don't let him have more than two treats a day. He'll get fat."

"Says?" My squeak got higher.

Death nodded, smiling fondly. "Oh, yes. They're all sentient and communicative. Quite charming."

Great. Take care of two dogs and a cat. Oh, by the way, they're faerie animals and can *talk*.

"Shouldn't be a problem?" I didn't mean for it to come out as a question, but at least Death ignored my linguistic slip. He just clapped his hands together and rose in one fluid motion, reminding me once again that no matter the fact he had pets, and talked about them like any normal human, he was an immortal being with grace and power. And if I hurt his pets, I would likely be snookered.

"Wonderful. Now, I don't leave until the morning, so just stop by the house around ten tomorrow and you should be just fine. Here are some instructions. I've left the food in the kitchen. If you have any problems, just get Yolanda to help you. She's looked after them before, and I would ask her again, but I rather think that she's afraid of Shakespeare. I can't think why."

Without so much as a toodle-oo, Death left. There was no more discussion of my current almost-Reaper status, nor any more instructions than that single sheet of paper on taking care of his animals. Just there one moment and gone the next. Leaving me stuck in the club chair, not from exhaustion, but from shock.

I, Cal Thorpe, was going to be responsible for *animals* for the next two to three days. Animals called Mischief, Mayhem, and Shakespeare. Oh, sure, this was going to go *swimmingly*.

I really wanted that pizza, now.

2

HERDING CATS

*Y*ou know how some days, no matter how prepared you are, things never seem to quite go the way you intended? Yeah, that was me on this particular Tuesday morning. My alarm went off as it usually does, demanding that I get up and get on with my day. As always, I tried to ignore it for all of thirty seconds before the tone sent me crazy. I turned it off, shuffled to the bathroom for a shower, and proceeded to discover that sometime during the night, the hot water had stopped working.

Three very cold minutes later, I jumped out and did my best to warm up by dressing in dark slacks, warm socks, a long-sleeved shirt and a thick sweater. It was not nearly so nice as my normal office attire. I, too, favoured suits, though I didn't have nearly as many as Death did, and my three-piece options had been destroyed during my recent adventures. As it turns out, running between Elsewhere and the mortal realms can be rather hard on the clothes.

The sweater—wool and silk in a nice dark green—helped, but only until I discovered that the coffee machine down in the office had gone out overnight, too.

I stared at the machine, feeling the full effect of the despondency that came along with it, until Yolanda shook my shoulder gently. Now, the thing about having a rock troll for an assistant was that while she was quite dogged in her pursuit of doing work—she could code quite well and had an impressive ability to winkle out information from people via the internet—she was also quite unaware how much stronger she was than normal people.

Yolanda was tall with greyish-green skin, large pointed ears that stuck out from the side of her head, bald, with a smile that was whiter than most toothpaste models. She was also built like a rugby player who had dipped into the anabolic steroids a few times. Compared to average-sized, average looking me with a decent (but not fantastic) physique, brown hair that truthfully needed a trim, and glasses, Yolanda was scary.

As it was, her gentle shake of my shoulders made my teeth rattle. I glanced up at her, putting all my despair over the lack of coffee into the look. "It broke," I said. "And the hot water's out."

Yolanda nodded. "Poltergeists. The wards around this building and Death's house are usually enough to keep them out, but they get through every now and again."

"But...the coffee." I waved my hand towards the machine. Yolanda tried to give me a pitying smile, but it didn't really work. While she didn't dislike coffee, popcorn was more her thing—rock trolls had an overt fondness for salt—and the microwave was still working.

"We can order delivery?" Yolanda suggested. I made a sound in the back of my throat. The coffee that I had in-house was a special blend created by a brownie whose kiosk I had visited in the Goblin Market. I had brokered a deal with her and now had a lifetime supply of coffee. It was, frankly, far superior to any other pitiful blend that I had tried, either here or in the mortal realms. I was working on widespread distribution potential with my marketing, but it hadn't yet reached the people it needed to reach.

I hadn't had the contract that long.

"While you do that, order a new coffee machine," I said. "See if those people here in Elsewhere can match the delivery speeds in the mortal realms. I hear they're getting things in a day!"

Yolanda shrugged and shuffled off to her desk to do as I asked, the bag of popcorn in the microwave popping merrily away. I grumbled. While Elsewhere had managed to do pretty much everything that could be done in the mortal realms, including social media, computers, marketing and the like, things like one-day delivery were still a ways off. I didn't understand it.

Surely, there were plenty of enterprising pixies or creatures who could run that would be happy to take up the mantle. Apparently, they already had jobs.

Centaur court runners, indeed.

Thinking of the courts reminded me of the fact that I was meant to be minding Death's pets for the next couple of days. I checked my clock; there was still time before I had to head over to the house and introduce myself to the animals. I eyed Yolanda, sitting hunched over at her desk as if waiting for a reprimand, and was about to head over to interrogate her on the three pets, when the door burst open and fell off its hinges, clattering to the floor.

Agravane stood there, glaring at the offending door. Being an aurai, he was possessed of the good looks and graceful movements that went with being a magical being. He wasn't quite so long-lived as some other beings out there—including myself, these days—but he had enough power to make him a relatively capable medium-weight hitter in the realm of Elsewhere. There were others who were actually immortal and looked quite a bit similar, but his power made up for lack of long life. This morning, though, Agravane's annoyingly good looks were marred by the fact that he was soaking wet.

His shirt, a nice light-blue number, had been torn to shreds, and the left leg of his slacks were gone. As he walked into the office, his shoes squelched.

I felt a mild interest in his appearance and my curiosity was only slightly louder. "So...?" I prompted, hoping that he would fill in the information. Instead, he just flicked his hands free of some water and trudged over to his desk, leaving wet shoe prints in his wake.

"I *hate* poltergeists," Agravane snarled. Yolanda nodded in agreement, looking up from her computer.

"Aurai and poltergeists are natural...well, not enemies. What's the word when you don't like each other and do what you can to annoy the other side and cause them problems but you don't actually try to kill each other?"

"Enemies," I said. "Just non-lethal enemies."

"They caught me with a patch of vines just as I was walking up the drive." Agravane reached up and pulled a leaf out of his wet hair. "And then they made it rain. Just on me!"

"They knocked out the coffee machine and the hot water, too," I said. Agravane glared at me, hunching his shoulders. He muttered something incoherent and went about stabbing at the keys of his computer. I turned back to Yolanda, deciding that it was safer to talk with her than to try and help the angry aurai who could probably kill me with a twist of his hands. Not that it would stick, but still.

"I'm pet sitting for Death while he's doing jury duty the next couple of days." I sidled up to her computer, casually looking over the screen to see if she'd ordered any coffee yet. All I saw were the usual social media sites that served the basis of our business. Yolanda jerked and widened her eyes at me, turtling her head between her shoulders. It was an odd look, considering she didn't have any real neck between her chin and shoulders on a normal day.

"Oh, Cal, you're not." Yolanda looked more than visibly alarmed at the prospect. I recalled that Death said he couldn't ask Yolanda again, but as she was scared of just about everything, despite being quite a bit larger and more dangerous than your average Elsewhere denizen, I hadn't thought much of it. Apparently, that though was incorrect.

"Death doesn't want to kennel them." I pulled out the instructions from my pocket, thinking of the last set of instructions that Death had given me. I ignored the riot of emotions that brought up, thinking of it a a cloud that passed momentarily over the sun. Just like that, the emotions were gone. A headache took their place. "Two dogs and a cat. I can surely manage that, can't I?"

"It's not just two dogs and a cat, Cal," Yolanda said. She pushed back from her desk and stood, walking over to me as if about to have a conversation that starts with "I'm concerned..."

"Okay, two sentient dogs and a cat." It might be nice to actually understand the animals.

"The dogs are alright, if a little over eager, but Shakespeare...he's insane, Cal!" Yolanda shivered. She darted past me and went straight for the popcorn, tearing open the bag and digging into it like candy. "The last time I took care of them, he said he wanted to play war games, and I was meant to be the attacking force. It took me *weeks* to heal, and I still have a scar on my back!"

I didn't know much about Faerie cats, but that did seem to track with the mortal felines.

"Well, I have to take care of them in any case. Death has likely already gone and I already agreed. If I just follow the instructions, then it shouldn't be too bad," I said. This time, I had made sure to read through all the instructions before embarking on this particular adventure. Life wouldn't be able to catch me by surprise this time. Granted, I doubted she had anything to do with the animals, but still. It wouldn't hurt to be prepared.

Even as I thought of Life, the forces within me writhed, trying to strangle each other. I closed my eyes and pushed the sensation aside, focusing instead on pleasant things like the weather, and wondering how poltergeists made it rain only on Agravane, and whether I would need a scarf now that it was getting cold out. When I opened my eyes, my emotions were controlled behind their opaque nature, and the tug-of-war had settled into the background.

Yolanda made a sound in the back of her throat and took her popcorn, cradled against her chest like a stuffed animal, back to her desk. I looked to Agravane for help, but he appeared to have ignored our conversation completely in exchange for stealing a towel from the bathroom to dry off. I checked my clock again and decided that I'd better leave before either one of them managed to talk me out of it.

I wandered out of the building that housed my offices and apartment and headed towards Death's mansion, avoiding the patch of vines and the singular floating raincloud that were still in the middle of the drive. Perhaps that was all that the poltergeists had planned. Though, I think depriving me of a hot shower and my morning coffee was more than enough to earn my ire. My eyes already drooped and my shoulders sagged; both completely physical reactions that had absolutely nothing to do with my emotions whatsoever and therefore were felt with the full effect of a typhoon.

Apparently, I hadn't gotten enough sleep last night.

Or the night before, or the one before that, going back two weeks.

I sighed and walked to the main house.

Death's mansion was reminiscent of the stately English country manor houses that were present in the mortal realms. The walls were made of hewn stone, the edges perfectly sculpted. The windows looked like leaded glass and the doors were surrounded by carved gargoyles and Green Men in various poses. There was ivy climbing up the walls, the silvery-grey variety that grew in Death's lands. The whole thing was surrounded by a haze of mist, making it look like something straight out of a gothic novel without any of the irony attached. It was, in a word, regal. And, I knew, it was actually comfortable inside, with wood pannel-ing, roaring fireplaces, a library full of books, furniture that was broken in and impossibly comfortable, pictures of pleasant scenery on the walls. Compared to the ultra-modern offices and old-world style apartment that I had been given upon my employment, Death's mansion felt like a singular piece of perfect architecture.

I entered the house and wiped my feet. I wasn't actually sure who managed the estate or kept the house clean, as I'd never seen any servants there, but I never liked to cause a mess just in case someone got mad. I wended my way to the kitchens, which, despite the rest of the house and it's old world style, was fully updated and modern. There, on the counter, in a box that was locked closed, was a collection of food and treats.

Sitting on top of the box, looking like it didn't have a care in the world, was the largest domestic cat I'd ever seen. It was all black, except for its white ears and the tip of its tail. Its fur was medium length and well-groomed, showing sleek muscles beneath. I couldn't quite tell by the way it was curled up, but its legs seemed longer than normal. It had yellow eyes with a vertical black slit and a single fang showed over its lip. All told, the thing was as big as my entire torso and must have weighed thirty pounds or so. It was, in a word, terrifying.

Then, it spoke. "You must be Calvin," the cat purred, the sound deep and vibrating in my ears like an earthquake. "Our temporary caretaker while the master is away attending to matters of justice."

"You're...you..." Apparently, actually coming to

terms with a cat that could talk was far more complicated than acknowledging its sentience. I would like to say that my jaw didn't fall open like some species of fish, but that would be a lie.

"I am Shakespeare, grimalkin and keeper of my master's house," the cat said. He stood and stretched, spine elongating and massive claws flashing as his paws churned the air. "You may acknowledge my magnificence, now."

"I...what? Oh, um, yes. Very impressive," I said, not quite sure if this was normal. Were all cats like this? I'd known they were generally considered aloof, but this seemed a bit extreme. "I was told that there were two dogs, too?"

Shakespeare flicked an ear and rolled his eyes. "Yes, those two idiots. Mischief and Mayhem are currently waiting at the back door for someone to let them out. I presume you wish to meet them."

Before I could say yes or no or even make any other movement, Shakespeare let out a *sound* that curdled my blood and sent shivers up my spine, muted emotion or no. It was like a yowl, but sharper, angrier, more demanding. There was magic in that sound and it was *beyond* dangerous. I don't know how I knew, but I knew.

Faerie cat? Scary.

Shakespeare sat neatly and wrapped his tail around his paws, wearing a disdainful look. "Here they come."

Indeed, the ground was now vibrating with movement. I heard the scrabbling of paws and claws over tile and wood and a moment later was bowled over by a force that seemed stronger even than Yolanda. I fell to the ground in a heap, staring wide-eyed up at the ceiling as two dark canine faces peered close to me, their tongues going for my chin.

I pushed them away—after several attempts and a good bathing, which smudged my glasses tremendously—and sat up, looking at what I was dealing with. Belgian Tervuren, Death had said. I assumed that was similar to a German Shepherd, because with their colouring and their long coats, they looked remarkably like the famous breed. Their ears were bigger, their nose more angular and their eyes were blood red. I doubted that last feature was common on a mortal dog. That would be the Fae blood.

"Ohmygoodnessyousmelllikepopcorn." One of the dogs, slightly smaller than the other and with more black on her body than brown, was wagging her tail so rapidly that her whole body shook. She tried to get close to me, her tongue lapping at my hand and revealing fangs that were definitely longer and sharper than mortal dog fangs.

"Mischief," Shakespeare said with a yawn, showing off his own wickedly dangerous teeth. He flicked his tail towards the other dog. "Mayhem."

Mayhem's tail was wagging, too, but slower. "Do you like to play ball?" he asked, nose twitching as he ran it over my trousers and the edge of my sweater. At the word "ball," Mischief stilled, every muscle freezing in place, only her eyes moving.

"Yes," she said with a single breath. "*Ball.*"

I blinked, looking around the kitchen for the ball chucker that Death had suggested. There it was, right next to the food container and just behind Shakespeare's noble bulk. The cat licked his muzzle. "This should be fun."

Okay, ball it was.

I grabbed the ball chucker.

It would prove, as ever, to be a mistake.

3

DOG TOYS

It turns out that when Shakespeare said "fun", what he meant was a very difficult time for the poor human trying to take care of the animals. Mischief and Mayhem leaped ahead of me and into the garden, running around the fenced in area with more speed than sense. Shakespeare settled into a patch of sun next to a plume of silvery grasses and proceeded to groom his paw, making sure to show off every claw. Meanwhile, I fumbled with the tennis ball and the throwing device.

As soon as the ball was in the plastic device, the dogs froze, their ears pricked and their attention turned on me. Mayhem inched closer, like he was stalking his prey. Mischief licked her chops. I raised the plastic arm. The dogs lowered their shoulders. I threw the ball and watched it soar.

Immediately, they were after it, running with speed that was probably more magical than mortal, though I had seen dogs run quite fast in various parks. They intercepted the path of the ball and neatly avoided colliding with each other, their paws blurring. Mayhem leaped first, jaws wide and teeth gleaming. The ball arced just a little farther and Mischief leaped, too, her body getting in the way of Mayhem's jump and ramming the other dog to the ground in a flash of dust.

Her jaws closed around the ball and she pirouetted on one paw, running back to me and dropping it at my feet. "*Ball*," she said.

Mayhem ran up a moment later, tongue lolling. "Throw again!"

Shakespeare yawned. "You're going to be here for hours, if you give in to their demands."

"My instructions are to exercise them," I pointed out, picking the ball up in the plastic chucker again. "This counts."

"I suppose," Shakespeare replied, whiskers twitching as I sent the ball flying again and the two dogs raced after it. "But it is rather dull. I thought that you were going to be more interesting. After all, you have such a complicated scent patterning. Instead, you just...throw the ball, like any hired fool."

I pulled the instructions out of my pocket and waved them at the cat. "What would you have me do? Ignore your master's requests that I take care of you? Not feed you? Not play with you? That doesn't seem to end in your favour, now does it?"

Shakespeare sighed and rolled onto his back, stretching one leg out and batting at a leaf that fell in his vicinity. "You have no imagination, Cal Thorpe. Never have I been so disappointed by a scent bouquet."

The dogs returned, this time Mayhem holding the ball in his jaws and Mischief dancing around him, whining piteously. Mayhem dropped the ball at my feet and sat, tail wagging in the dirt. "Throw *again*."

I was beginning to feel my annoyance—mostly at Shakespeare—rise like a thundercloud, threatening to ruin what looked to be a decent day. All I had to do was play with the dogs, feed them, make sure they were attended. I had to feed Shakespeare, pet him when he demanded. It should have been a nice, normal day. After the last few weeks that I'd had, I really needed a nice, normal day. Even poltergeists weren't going to dampen my mood.

Shakespeare yawned vocally, sitting up. "If you're going to be a bore, at least make them work for it. I might as well enjoy their frivolous efforts. Aim for that back left corner, oh boring human."

Poltergeists paled in comparison to being sneered at by a superior know-it-all of a cat.

I grabbed the ball with the throwing arm and wound my arm back as far as it would go, trying to remember my days as a cricket player in school. I hadn't been particularly good at bowling, but I had been decent. And right now, anger counted a lot more than skill. I released my arm forwards and let the ball fly, the yellow-green projectile soaring higher and farther than before.

Shakespeare snickered.

The dogs shot off after the all, their whole bodies expanding and contracting as they stretched their paws before them, digging into the ground and pushing themselves forward. The ball kept going and I waited for one of them—Mischief, maybe—to surge upwards and snatch it from the air. Only, she didn't. And the ball? It kept going.

Right over the fence.

Niether dog hesitated. Mayhem pushed his back legs into the ground and surged over the fence in a single, fluid motion. Mischief leaped to a boulder and spring-boarded off of it over the fence. With a flurry of wagging tails, they vanished into the tall grass on the other side of Death's garden.

I just stood there for a moment, half waiting for them to come leaping back over the fence and drop the ball at my feet. They didn't. "Um...are they going to come back?" I asked Shakespeare. The cat chuckled, his shoulders roiling with the motion.

"I was wrong about you," Shakespeare said, rising to his feet. He wound around my leg, his shoulder coming to my knee. He looked up at me with a wicked gleam in his eye. "You have no imagination. But you're still very fun, and you follow directions nicely. I think we'll get along well enough."

"That'd be a no, then." I turned and went back inside, depositing the ball chucker on the kitchen counter and cursing. Loudly. I pulled out the instructions and read fervently, hoping that there was something I had missed. Like some magical chant to get the two dogs to come back. Instead, there was just a little notation at the bottom of the page, just where Death liked to put all of his really important information:

Try not to let the dogs get out. They have a bad habit of running off when not on the leash or in the garden.

I snarled and stuffed the paper back into my pocket. Shakespeare was sitting on the counter, his paws neatly tucked together, just barely touching two retractable leashes next to a pouch of treats. I jabbed my finger towards the cat and he pulled his head back, flicking his white ears. "You're going to help me get them back."

"And why in the world would I do something like that? I'm not beholden to you." To prove his point, he yawned.

"You're going to do it because you like to be entertained. You're going to do it because I'm meant to be taking care of you for the next two to three days and am *not* going to leave you here alone; I'm not that dumb. You're going to do it because if you don't, I will put you in a tiny cat carrier and deliver you, personally, to Yolanda to take care of." I was inches away from the cat's face when I finished my demands, my teeth bared in what I hoped was a terrifying expression. Shakespeare blinked slowly, looking more bored than anything.

He took in a deep breath, looked around, and then sighed as if I had just demanded the world of him. "Oh, very well. I swear to accompany you and assist you in your endeavours to reacquire Mischief and

Mayhem, those two buffoons. Will that be satisfactory?"

"Say it again," I said in a low voice. "Twice."

Shakespeare pricked his ears. "Well, well, I *am* impressed. You know more about faeries than you let on."

After my last experience with the creatures—involving a dying girl, some food and a witch—I had done some research on Faeries, or the Fae. I didn't know much, only that they were divided into courts of Seelie and Unseelie, both associated with different seasons and pieces of nature. I knew they didn't like iron, had to tell the truth—though they could bend their words like master liars—and that you could only bind them into an agreement if they swore three times.

"Swear," I said flatly.

"I swear, I swear. There you have it, three times said," Shakespeare huffed. He leaped off the counter and wandered to the back door. "Now, are you coming or not?"

I grabbed the leashes and the bag of treats, sticking all of them in a paper bag with handles, and followed after the massive, scary, cat. Shakespeare moved along like some sort of shadow, blending in to the darker pieces of Death's lands. His ears and the tip of his tail were often the only things that gave him away, twitching and acting like beacons to draw me forwards. I was normally fully capable with the silvery blue-grey landscape, the quiet fog and the sense of grey that permeated the lands. I had grown used to them and even fond of them. After many of my "adventures" as Yolanda liked to put it, I spent time just taking in the vastness and the quiet of the trees and the fields. I had, on occasion, also walked the areas around my house and Death's mansion, taking advantage of the neat trails that wended there.

I hadn't, though, trudged cross-country into the abyss after two dogs who would not, no matter how often I called, respond to their names. It felt very strange to be calling out, "Mischief, Mayhem!" so after a while, I let my calls fade away and just followed the cat farther and farther into the depths of Death's lands.

"I've never been this far in," I said after we had gone nearly half a mile. Shakespeare leaped lightly from a moss-covered boulder to a protruding tree root and then to what looked like a game trail cutting right through the middle of the woods. "I usually go to the other end, where it borders—"

"Yes, yes, you're quite new at this, you want information, all that nonsense. You're really quite loud enough without adding conversation to the mix. Perhaps we could just focus on walking, hmm?" Shakespeare asked, not even bothering to look over his shoulder at me. I rolled my eyes at his back and tripped over a root. The cat snickered at me and just kept going.

Arrogant monster.

I regained my balance, at least slightly glad that I had worn—for once—a pair of shoes that I could walk in. Most of the time, my little excursions ended up ruining my shoes as well as my suits. This time, figuring I would be playing with the dogs, I had worn a pair of dark, lace up trainers. They didn't match my slacks at all, but they at least handled the soggy leaves and other undergrowth quite well. My sweater, on the other hand, kept getting snagged by twigs and bark. I only hoped it wouldn't unravel.

Seriously, I needed a raise just to handle all the clothes that kept getting destroyed by my jobs for Death and Life.

After a long while of following behind Shakespeare, occasionally tripping over something and managing, barely, not to smash my face on the ground, I did notice something strange. The forest that we had been wandering through was changing colour, and getting thicker.

I don't know if you've ever been in an old-growth hardwood forest anywhere in England or Europe. If you haven't, then let me tell you: it is something to behold. The trees seem to have spaced themselves out nearly perfectly. There is space to wander beneath them, the undergrowth that survives is mostly ferns or ivy, thanks to the lack of light. There is usually a thick blanket of leaves that covers the ground and a person can travel quite well for a good long distance.

The problems of stumbling through undergrowth-infested forest with huge numbers of trees that get in your way and try to keep you from moving forwards comes when you reach the younger parts of the forest, the parts where each plant and tree is still vying for dominance. The edges of the forest or the places around glades are like this.

This new forest was like an old-growth collection of hardwoods had suddenly decided to start waging war against one another. There were massive, well-spaced trees and a blanket of leaves underfoot. But there were also smaller, more agressive trees surrounded by a whole collection of ivies and ferns and wildflowers, grasses, weeds, tangled goldenrod, tansy, you name it. It was a forest on steroids.

The colours, too, were different. The silvers and blues and greys and washed-out greens of Death's lands shifted to something far more saturated and vibrant, showing off autumn colours to their full extent. It wasn't anything quite like the pure intensity of colour that surrounded Life's lands, just somehow more than you would expect from a forest.

Altogether, this was a forest that absolutely knew it was a forest, right in the middle of its autumn cycle, no less, despite the rest of Elsewhere being right at the end of that season. Amidst all the undergrowth and trees, there was a single path to follow and inevitably, Shakespeare and I ended up on it. The cat flattened his ears as some creature called out across the forest. It sounded like a bird, but was perhaps ten degrees more vicious.

"Are you sure this is the right way?" I asked, being sure to keep my voice low. Shakespeare said nothing, just kept sauntering on like he owned the forest and everything in it. I followed on after him, feeling more and more put out by all of this. These dogs, when we found them, were going to get a piece of my mind. And then I was going to punish them by promising not to throw the ball for the rest of my time taking care of them. It would serve them right.

I stumbled, nearly losing my glasses as I windmilled my arms to regain my balance. Shakespeare rammed his shoulder into my lower leg and I stumbled backwards, no longer in any danger of falling over, though I would definitely have a bruise there later. The cat sat, licking his chest fur. After a moment, he flicked his tail towards a small stream that crossed over the path.

"We have to go that way. Their scent trail leads directly over it," Shakespeare mewed. I nodded, hefting the paper bag in my hand and started forwards. The faerie cat darted a paw out and caught his claws in the edge of my trousers, pulling me back with almost as much force as the shoulder check.

"Geez, what's that about," I grumbled, shaking my leg to disentangle his claws. "If we have to go that way, we go that way."

"How can you be so knowledgeable in some things and so idiotic in others?" Shakespeare rose to his paws and dug his claws into the soil. "Mischief and Mayhem don't get out on their own very often; one, because Death isn't stupid enough to walk them without a leash; and two, because they actually obey him when he calls. You, on the other hand, are just a temporary caretaker and so they are bound to test their boundaries."

"*They*'re testing their boundaries?" I scoffed. "You've been testing them all day!"

Shakespeare sighed, sides heaving. "No, stupid human, I haven't. I am naturally this contrary. Trust me, when I test my boundaries, you will know it."

Great. Just what I needed. I rubbed the back of my neck with my free hand. "Okay, so, what? They're testing their boundaries and going for a run through Elsewhere."

Shakespeare jabbed his tail at the stream. "No, they're running straight to Faerie. Think of it like...catnip. All Faerie creatures are drawn there. It is our nature."

Something in his eyes gleamed as he said this, and I was suddenly conscious of the smell of blood and decay. I knew almost nothing about grimalkins, except that they were Faerie cats and often heralded or involved death. I was fairly certain that I didn't want to know the sort of death they congregated around.

"Okay, so we go get them back," I said, once again starting forwards. "I've been loads of places in Elsewhere. I've even dealt with Faeries. I don't see how this is going to be any different."

The cat stretched and shook his pelt, the black fur glimmering in the light, looking so much more black than it had done before. I knew this was an effect of Faerie, making things seem more "real", more how they "should" be. It was, apparently, dangerous for normal humans to spend much time there. Not that I was normal.

"Very well, Cal Thorpe. We will venture into Faerie and retrieve Death's dogs. But do not say I didn't warn you out of the goodness of my heart. Things in Faerie are not as they seem, and you will require *all* your wiles to survive." With that, Shakespeare leaped across the boundary stream, his fur sticking out on end, his tail twice its size. With his chest puffed up and a feral gleam in his eyes, Shakespeare looked like he would happily have killed someone and then gone on to feast on their entrails. He looked like a being out of legend, one meant to stalk you in the dark and haunt your nightmares.

Whereas, when I stepped over the stream, I accidentally slipped on the bank and got my left shoe wet. I was still flicking off the mud when were were surrounded by creatures pointing spears at us.

"Figures," was all I said as I raised my hands into the air. Shakespeare eyed me, one ear pointing in my direction.

"You expected this?" he asked, voice low.

"Well, nothing in this job is ever *easy*, is it?"

The cat started sniggering as the warriors closed in. I didn't even get a chance to explain myself before one of them reached out with a silver-tipped spear and sliced through my throat. Nope, never easy, this job.

4

BEWARE OF DOG

*A*gravane had been pestering me for quite some time, now, about learning self-defence, because even though I couldn't be killed, I could be maimed. Which sucked. And, while I hadn't had more than a couple weeks' worth of training from him, I knew enough to duck out of the way of people trying to kill me.

So, I leaned my shoulders back and instead of taking a good portion of my throat with it, the spear just grazed my skin enough to bleed maybe a trickle. It wouldn't be enough to stain my sweater. It still hurt, paper-cut style. Figures.

"Hold, fool creature!" Shakespeare snarled, his voice somehow becoming sharper, more dangerous, like he was somehow more feral, more intelligent on this side of the stream than the other. Given that he was a grimalkin, a Faerie cat, it was distinctly possible. I'd been told that the Fae of Elsewhere were so bound by their nature that they often seemed more solid, more real, more true, than anything conceived by the mortal realm. Right now, that meant Shakespeare was not only more vicious, but also possessed of astronomical amounts of arrogance. With a yowl, he leaped in front of me and bared his teeth.

The five or so creatures surrounding us took a step back. They were long-limbed things with unruly, ivy-like hair and eyes that took up a good portion of their face. They wore clothes that seemed to be some mix of plant matter and leather, the spears in their hand the only metal on them. One hissed at Shakespeare, revealing mildly pointed teeth. The cat hissed back, the sound causing the creature to yelp and scramble away.

"Great malk," another creature said, this one with a grassy beard, "what brings you to venture into Faerie with a mortal trespasser?"

"Do you always try to kill those that entire your domain? I thought the Fae of the cold courts, the Winter and the Darkness, were smarter than that." Shakespeare sat and proceeded to lick a paw, acting as if these creatures were anything but a threat to him. He lifted his chin defiantly. "I thought it was your practise to take mortals for entertainment, for sport. Yet you just kill without question?"

The bearded creature clicked its teeth together. "These are perilous times, noble malk. We are tasked to keep careful control over our borders. Watch for intruders. Even you, a member of our court by blood, would not necessarily be welcomed here, not without good reason."

I opened my mouth to explain our purpose there and yelped instead. Shakespeare pulled his claws out of the soft toes of my shoe and I was suddenly wishing that I had worn my leather ones, even if it meant ruining another pair. I'd much rather have my toes in one piece, as opposed to shredded by cat claws.

"We are here on a quest," Shakespeare announced, holding his head high, his nose in the air. The creatures shuffled and muttered excitedly to one another in a language that I didn't understand and didn't want to understand. It sounded like the cracking of ice and promised a good deal of bother. These days, I was not in the mood for bother. "We seek that which belongs to my master, which strayed over your border. We seek an audience with your queen."

"And who is your master, malk, that you would dare demand such a boon?" the creature spat. Dispensing with the formalities was never a good sign.

"Death." Shakespeare said it in such a way that you would have thought he was just tossing out random words, things that had no meaning, no purpose, and that no one would care about. It was casual, said with a flick of his ear and a languid blink.

The Faerie creatures all hissed as one.

"The queen will want to see you," the leader said after adjusting his spear in his grip. He eyed me. "Is the mortal necessary to your plans?"

Shakespeare considered me, licking his jaws as he

yawned. I returned the look, glaring. "I suppose he has some useful qualities."

"Very well. Then we had better get to the Hall. Come, we move swift for fear our enemies attack," the thing said. It waved its spear and the creatures started running off. Shakespeare bounded after them. I sighed, tried not to think about how terrible running was for the joints, and jogged after them, the paper bag with the dog leashes bouncing against my side.

I caught up with Shakespeare. "What's all this about enemies?"

Shakespeare leaped over a massive fallen tree crossing the path. I scrambled up one side and tripped down the other before resuming the jog. At least the path ahead was relatively clear.

"The Fae are divided into courts. Traditionally, Summer and Winter, along the Seelie and Unseelie boundaries, but within each there are factions that claim things like Autumn or Spring or Darkness and Light. It is like...well think of it like the European monarchy, with their royal families, their noble houses. They are, as their nature would suggest, locked in opposition. We are in Winter territory, now. And those are beings of the Dark. Plantlings. Not quite as dangerous as, say, me, but certainly plenty capable for border guards. Though why so many, I do not know. The Fae are not yet at war."

I saved myself from faceplanting into a puddle and Shakespeare sighed audibly. I decided not to ask about this war. I just wanted to stay long enough to get the dogs back. As far as I was concerned, the Fae could deal with each other as they chose. Shakespeare's interest, though, was unsettling. I really hoped this would be a simple task. I knew, though, that it would be something far more complicated. It always was.

As we went in, the trees and forest around us became more shadowed, colder. The autumn that we had encountered at the edge of the border was still present in the way that all the plants were in full autumn colours, some flowers even in late bloom, but it was an impossible growth considering that I was beginning to feel like my fingers had been thrown into an industrial freezer, despite the jogging. The plants became covered with a hoarfrost and I nearly slipped twice on patches of ice beneath the leaves on the path. Shakespeare's coat was somehow fuller, shaggier, and the plantlings were *growing* new tendrils to wrap around themselves.

Right. Winter.

And I hadn't even brought gloves.

Then, we came upon a clearing. It was more than a clearing, really, with a massive hill and an expanse of clear land that stretched a good ways around the hill. Topping the hill was what looked like a castle. And I don't mean one of those fancy Disney style castles that are fanciful and have magnificent architecture, like Neuschwanstein. I mean a fortress, meant to keep out a sieging army for days, weeks, even months at a time.

It had an outer wall that was three times my height, with tiny slits in the stone for people to fire arrows out of. The top of the wall had crenelations in the shape of snowflakes that would hide any guards or people aiming to pour pitch and fire on their attackers. The inner wall stretched taller than the outer wall, with another set of positions for guards. Then, there was the castle, a building that took up a goodly portion of the interior of the walls, stretching tall and imposing on a poor marketing expert who just wanted to get some dogs and go home.

As soon as the plantlings, Shakespeare and I stepped into the open, I felt every set of eyes on the top of those walls turn and stare at me. I was suddenly hyper-conscious that I had a line of blood around my neck. Dried or no, it was basically waving a banner in the face of these predators that I was closer to prey.

Cheerful thoughts, Cal, I thought. *They could have already shot me by now.*

5

A DOG'S LIFE

Weirdly enough, given that I'm just a marketing schmuck, I've been in a lot of castles-slash-palaces-slash-mansions. Death lived in a manor house, sure, but it was far and away grander than most mortal manors. And Life? She lived in a palace. Even discounting those two, I'd been in a castle owned by vampires, a true Renaissance palazzo (also owned by vampires), a ridiculously expensive apartment in Chicago owned by a mobster...you see my point.

Anyways, I'm fairly certain that the castle throne room or whatever to where Shakespeare and I had been dragged was meant to impress. It had huge, vaulted ceilings with massive wooden beams running across it, various scenes of magical and Faerie life carved into them. The windows were large and let in an enormous amount of light, all shining directly on the tapestries that adorned the walls and the courtiers that adorned the floor. The members of the Faerie court, or courts, were beings that ranged from human-like, only exceptionally beautiful and predatory, to things that looked to be sculpted from shadow or stone. They all wore finery of some sort, varying in historical accuracy and number of ridiculous and sparkly adornments with the most dramatic ones being closer to the throne. It would have been, to almost anybody else, a very impressive sight.

I was more interested in the various exits around the room, and the fact that Mischief and Mayhem were sitting at the feet of a stunningly beautiful woman with cat-slitted eyes of ice and a sword of a gleaming blue metal. The dogs had their heads on their paws and their ears lowered.

"Greetings, my queen!" The lead plantling sidled close to the throne, shoving courtiers out of the way as he stumbled into a low bow. The other plantlings followed his lead. Shakespeare and I just stood there, slightly behind the plantlings and surrounded by courtiers who, I'm fairly certain, could tear us apart with their pinky fingers. "We bring you trespassers from the border with the Lands of Silence."

The queen straightened, her white hair crackling with the movement, as though it had been frozen. This, I gathered, was the Winter Queen, leader of the Unseelie faeries and a dangerous person. At her side was a man, also lethally beautiful, who was sitting on a slightly lower throne. He looked a little bored. The

Winter King, then, a being who would lead their forces into battle, if battle ever came.

I knew only a tiny bit about the Unseelie versus Seelie line of division, but one thing I did know was that the Fae before me were considered cruel, vindictive, malicious, even evil. The Seelie, by comparison, were considered quite benevolent.

Neither, I think, were all that inclined to be nice to mortals.

"The Lands of Silence," the queen said, her voice rolling over me like a wave of pure cold. It was the sort of thing that would knock you down if you weren't careful. I wasn't careful, but I at least knew enough to brace my weight against magical onslaught. "How very interesting. I haven't had visitors from Death's lands in many decades, and now, all of a sudden, I have several in one day. What do you think of that, my love?"

The king slid forwards in his throne and leaned over a knee to look at us. Frost rolled off of him in a cresting wave, extending towards us with almost palpable curiosity. Shakespeare sat, calmly wrapping his tail around his paws and flicking his ears. Given that he was a cat, I doubted very much that he would be concerned by any sort of royalty. That was confirmed when he yawned. I, on the other hand, just stood there and tried not to move my head and reopen the cut on my neck.

The king's gaze was intense, calculating. An image flashed into my mind of me running through the middle of the forest while he chased me down like a hunted animal or an enemy warrior. He wanted blood, and mine would do. I blinked and the image vanished. Mind games, was it? How very like a gust of wind. Annoying for a brief moment and then quickly forgotten.

I really needed to stop comparing my emotional state to the weather.

"Do we bore you, grimalkin?" the queen asked, frost brewing around her hands.

Shakespeare twitched his tail. "Bore us? Oh, no, my magnificent queen. We are not bored, merely weary from our long journey through the lands of my master, here on a quest to retrieve my companions, those same hounds that lay at your feet."

"I expect more quickness of tongue from you, grimalkin. Do you not share the name of a bard who tried to tame us to the page?" The queen sat back in her chair, her teeth flashing as she smiled. I noticed that they were sharp. All of them.

Shakespeare flattened his ears. "My name was given to me as a translation into this poor approxima-tion of our language, long before the time of that defiant man. Not from any particular similarity in tongue, dear queen. To be named after a human, a mere mortal, who had the audacity to write about Faeries as if he were all knowing, diminishing us to the mischievous likes of the Seelie court..." The cat shook his head. "I cannot control translation."

The queen tossed back her head, hair cracking, and laughed, the sound brittle and bringing a couple of icicles hanging off the back of her throne crashing to the ground. "You may not have quite as much poetry, but your tongue is quick enough, malk. I can see why my guards let you through when they should have killed you on sight."

The plantlings shrivelled—literally—under the sharp gaze of their queen. They all muttered something in their chattering, harsh tongue, and backed off, bowing obsequiously as they got out of her sight. A tall courtier who looked like she was made from a tree, and much more elegantly than the plantlings at that, snickered as they fled.

"I'm not sure killing us would have been all that great an idea," I said, deciding that maybe I should argue for our lives if no one else was going to do so. Every head in the room—including Shakespeare's—whipped in my direction. Mischief raised her head from the ground an inch and I saw her tail give the barest of wags.

"A human!" The queen clapped her hands, pieces of ice flaking off her skin as she did. She grinned eagerly at me and ran her tongue over her teeth. "How quaint. Shakespeare, my dear malk, it has been so long since a human not bound to me has graced this court. Such...potential lies before him, though I see blood both ahead and behind him. Is he a gift?"

Shakespeare bared his teeth at me, silently commanding me to keep quiet. I could easily have done so, but I'd had enough of people trying to manipulate me into being what they wanted. Even these few Faeries were so sure that I wasn't what I was, who I was, that they just dismissed me as a useless mortal, good only for entertainment. Blood indeed.

I'd kept quiet in the past, knowing that walking into a situation without a full grasp of the facts was just as dangerous as running around with a sword, screaming. It had served me well, generally speaking, letting me gather more information and therefore learn how to deal with whatever obstacles came my direction in a normal, rational manner. Keeping quiet had also involved other people speaking for me, making statements about me, even going so far as to make decisions for me.

Look where that had landed me.

So I ignored Shakespeare and, despite all my better judgement whispering loudly in my ears, I spoke. "Ha ha," I said drily. "How very amusing."

The Winter queen sat back in her chair, her spine ramrod straight and her icy eyes narrowed. "Amusing?"

I nodded, putting my hands into my pockets and effecting a casual stance. "Indeed. Oh, I know that it's all part of the big show. You have your role to play in the story of the world and you've been cast as the, well, not the *bad guy*, per se, but certainly someone more mischievous, dark, closer to Death. After all, your lands border the Lands of Silence."

"And what do you know of Death, tiny human?" the king asked, his expression turning more shark-like the longer he looked at me. A hunter, if the vision I had seen was any indication.

I bowed my head and pressed a hand to my chest, the picture of false humility. "I am but his humble servant. No, I get it, I really do! You have a role to fulfil. Faeries are all about roles, aren't they. That's why there are two courts: Seelie and Unseelie. You have archetypes to adhere to and in this particular instance, your archetype—the overlord with an iron fist, even if it is in a beautiful, velvet glove—requires that an example be made, or a gift provided to appease your wrath, and you expect the poor, innocent mortal to play that part. That's what we're for, isn't it?"

The courtiers had, initially, been whispering amongst each other at the start of my speech, but they now fell completely silent. Even Shakespeare didn't deign to twitch a muscle, his eyes wide and staring, his ears and tail perfectly still. I made sure that everyone was watching me when I narrowed my eyes a fraction of an inch at the Winter queen.

"In this instance, your majesty, you are quite wrong."

A single creature gasped, some small, fur-covered creature wielding a battle-axe. The queen's right hand reacted faster than I could follow, the limb flashing out and a single finger pointing at the creature. A wave of pure, impossible cold flowed out from that single point and the creature froze solid.

No one else said anything.

"All I want," I continued, "is to collect Death's property and return to his lands." I pointed at Mischief and Mayhem, making eye contact with each. Then, I pointed at my feet. A command. A demand.

The dogs, ears flat against their heads and their tails tucked between their legs, obeyed. They were halfway down the two steps that led to me when the Winter queen's voice snapped out and stopped them in their tracks.

"Stop!" she said, tone searing. The dogs stopped. "These two, part Fae though they may be, trespassed on our lands. Given that we Faeries must fulfil certain roles into which the world has cast us—" she fixed me with a glacial smile, "—I cannot simply *give* them two you."

I sighed, raising my brows and trying not to look annoyed by the proceedings. So much for abject confidence. "And what price would be required for their safe return. And our own freedom?" I pointed at Shakespeare and I, making sure to include everything I could think of into the bargain. Many easily-avoidable scandals in the marketing world would have passed everyone by if someone had bothered to actually make appropriate agreements. Or, well, not do stupid things to begin with, but we were way beyond that point.

The queen tapped her chin with her finger, leaving residual shards of ice in their wake. "You are an amusing mortal, for all that you trespassed here. Therefore, if you can but complete one task for me, then I shall grant you and your companions' freedom from our lands."

Great. I scratched my nose. A quest. How absolutely bothersome. I thought I'd be done with quests for a good long while. Simple tasks, maybe even a couple of marketing conference calls, were all I had hoped to deal with for a while. I'd hoped that fetching lunch for the office would be the closest I'd come to a quest, at least until I got a raise, or until Life demanded some ridiculousness of me. But, no.

"What is this task?" I asked, already feeling resignation creep into my spine. It must have been quite strong to actually make itself known in the slump of my shoulders.

"Oh, no. Agreement, then I tell you. I know you, mortal. You would try to be tricky with me."

I glanced at Shakespeare, who pointedly turned his attention away from me and started grooming a paw. He chewed on a claw, emphasising his annoyance. Fine, it was up to me. Well, given all the things I'd experienced in the last year and a half, I figured a Faerie quest would be right in the middle on the scale of difficulty.

"Fine." I waited.

"Swear. Thrice." She leaned forwards expectantly, a pool of frost spreading from her feet in her eagerness.

"I swear, I swear, I swear to complete this task in exchange for thrice sworn freedom and safe passage for me and my companions." I folded my arms.

"And I swear, promise, and oblige myself to grant you and your companions freedom in exchange for the completion of the task I set to you," the queen said. At the completion of her words, the courtiers started clapping enthusiastically, some even going so far as to whistle. The Winter queen sank back on her throne with a smug smirk.

"Cal, you are an absolute, inimitable, complete idiot," Shakespeare said.

Mischief and Mayhem took that moment to run to me and wag their tails as hard as they could, shaking their whole bodies in the process. "Oh, *thank you thank you*," Mischief said, thrusting her head under my hand so I could scratch her ears.

"Staying in Faerie would be *bad*," Mayhem agreed, pressing his shoulder into my knee so that the limb almost buckled.

"Idiots. The lot of you." Shakespeare lifted his nose into the air.

The queen clapped once and the hall silenced again, awaiting her proclamation. "You, ah...your name, please?"

I looked at Shakespeare, who shrugged, presumably giving me permission. "Cal," I said simply. If she were a good researcher, she could figure out who I was just from that and the knowledge that I worked for Death, but at least she wouldn't have my full name from my own tongue. Apparently that was a Bad Thing in some parts of Elsewhere.

"Very well, Cal. You shall, in accordance with our agreement, venture into the lands of our rival Summer court and retrieve an object."

Murmured gasps and exclamations broke out, as if

the queen had just suggested something incredibly dangerous and terrible for me to do. As far as I could tell, it was simple theft. Presumably surrounded by all sorts of obstacles and things that would try to kill me, but a simple theft nonetheless. I shrugged.

"What's this object?" I asked.

"A piece of jewellery." The Winter queen waved her hand dismissively. "My servant will tell you when you arrive in the Summer lands."

Now it was my turn to mutter and gasp, though it came out more like a grumble. "Your servant?"

"Indeed. I must trust you to return in a timely manner, and to retrieve the object that I tell you. Sworn you may be, but I still don't trust you, Cal."

I mean, she had a point.

The queen waved her hand towards the back of the room and I felt, more than saw, the courtiers behind me shuffling around to make room for this servant of the Winter queen. I was expecting a massive ice troll or maybe a red cap, even a fetch. What I got instead was a woman. A human woman.

She stopped next to me without looking in my direction, her entire focus on the Winter queen. She was tall, black skinned, and built like a MMA fighter. She wore some sort of tunic over buckskin breeches, leather boots lacing up to her shins. Her arms were bare, despite the cold, and a tattoo in a bright, reality-defying silver snaked up one arm, across the back of her neck, and down the other arm. The tattoo was of a monster being slain by some sort of warrior—probably viking-age—with a sword and a fur mantle.

I recognised the story, though the fact that I did was something surprising in itself. I wasn't very good with art, let alone remembering myths and legends. Though, I had improved in that last aspect in my current employment. Myths and legends had a nasty habit of jumping out to scare you. The story that this woman had tattooed on her was that of Beowulf and Grendel.

Good times.

"Dagmar, meet Cal." The queen swept her hand towards me and the slightly-terrifying woman turned towards me, inclining her head, as if she had just been given permission to acknowledge that I existed. "He is going to accompany you to retrieve that object from the court of our enemies."

Dagmar's brown eyes widened and her nostrils flared. She looked like she wanted to protest, loudly, but said nothing, merely inclining her head again. "As you say, my queen," she said, clasping her fists to her chest and bowing.

I shrugged and stuffed my hands into my pockets. "Right, so we'll be on our way, just after we drop Mischief, Mayhem and Shakespeare at the border."

The Winter queen smiled. Then, she pressed a hand to her mouth just before she burst out laughing. "You are far more naive than you thought, Cal! Perhaps you are nothing more than a regular mortal. At least your death will be of great entertainment to us!"

It took me a moment to understand what the queen was saying, but Mischief whined and pressed her shoulder into my leg. Mayhem put his ears back. Neither of them made a move towards the exit. Even Shakespeare hadn't moved at my proclamation that we would drop them off at the border.

"Right," I cursed to myself, "I forgot to put an immediate release date into the agreement."

They were staying here while I retrieved this jewellery.

Dagmar threw me a look from the corner of her eye, but said nothing. She just stood there, as if waiting for her next order from the queen. The tattoo on her arm flashed almost white, then shifted back to silver. If I hadn't known better than to take anything that happened in Elsewhere for granted, I would have assumed it was nothing more than a trick of the light. I tried to figure out just how to get the animals back to Death's lands so that they couldn't be used against me, or Death.

"Mischief and Mayhem will remain here to grace your court with their ferocity and prowess," Shakespeare said, stretching and rising to his feet. "I, in the mean time, will accompany my foolish mortal companion to be sure that he does not die too quickly and thus deprive you of your entertainment."

The courtiers snickered, eyeing me as though I couldn't possibly survive very long. Dagmar, on the other hand, looked like she could handle just about anything, and I didn't even see any obvious weapons on her person. It was fine. With my average height, average looks, glasses, and what Yolanda and Agravane called my "cute angry face", I was pretty used to being underestimated. It was much better than being overestimated, I had to admit.

I said nothing. Maybe it was time to let Shakespeare actually assist, considering he did know the Fae better. I had run my mouth already today; I wasn't sure the universe could handle more than that.

"Very well, malk," the queen said, waving her fingers at Shakespeare as if he were nothing more than a nuisance. I saw the cat bristle at the tone and couldn't blame him. Being dismissed as a nuisance was far worse than being underestimated.

I knelt down to scratch Mischief and Mayhem behind the ears and under the chins, earning a half-hearted tail wag from each. "Hey, I know that staying here isn't ideal, but you two are smart and capable, right? You just wait here and I'll be back for you. And if I'm not, then Death most certainly will be."

"Okay," Mischief murmured.

Mayhem stuck his head against my chest and was slightly less emotional. "Ball," he whispered. I sighed and dug into the bag at my side, handing him the ball. I handed the handles of the bag to Mischief, who took them gently in her teeth. Both dogs looked at me like I was never going to return.

I stood, earning another strange look from Dagmar, though she continued to keep her mouth shut. I wondered if she would keep quiet during our journey and just communicate through her quite vivid facial expressions. It would be an interesting trip, if that were the case, and certainly novel for me to have a non-communicative companion.

Then again, I was stuck with Shakespeare as tagalong. I would probably be lectured at length on how much of an idiot I was.

"You may go," the Winter queen said, leaning back into her throne and resting her hands on the arms. "And remember: we will be watching."

"Watching?!" I managed to splutter the one word before the castle, the court, and all the art fell away into nothingness and dark, tangled forest appeared in its place. There was a definite chill in the air, and I could see frost on my glasses. Shakespeare and Dagmar were at my sides, Shakespeare's tail twice the size it was usually. He frantically started to lick it down into shape and Dagmar muttered something under her breath, tattoo shifting slightly, as if the characters depicted disliked the situation.

"What does she mean, watching?"

"Just that," Dagmar said, pulling out a knife from the small of her back. "The Unseelie will watch us with a scrying spell. They cannot hear us, but they will get a great deal of entertainment from watching. I imagine there will be several bargains made and lost on this journey."

"Great, just great. I'm the subject of betting, have to travel to a Faerie court known for being only slightly less bothersome than the one I just left, and have Miss

Optimist to join me." I started stalking off in the only direction that seemed at least mildly clear of tangling encumbrances.

"Oh, Cal?" Shakespeare asked. I spun on my heel and glared.

"What?"

"You're going the wrong way."

6

SCAREDY CAT

*A*s it turns out, even high-end trainers were unsuitable footwear for delving deep into the middle of Faerie territory. By the time we'd made it perhaps two miles—which Dagmar graciously informed me was an extremely slow pace, set by yours truly here—my shoes had been torn to pieces by thorny vines, muddy puddles, and an overzealous squirrel. The sun was beginning to set and I was beginning to feel hunger.

"You could have at least asked for supplies," Shakespeare grumbled after pouncing and killing a pitifully tiny mouse. He stared at the morsel distastefully then ate it with great delicacy, ignoring the piercing glare that Darmar gave him for not moving. "I prefer my food cooked."

"Death spoils you," I said, shaking my left foot to get rid of some migrating mushroom that had decided my ruined shoe was a perfect place to rest. "No wonder you're so big."

"It's muscle," Shakespeare complained. He swallowed down the rest of the mouse and then started leaping forwards again, his paws barely seeming to touch the ground, let alone get tangled in all the debris that was clogging my way. "And I resent your implication."

"Resent away," I said. I made it about ten feet before a tree branch appeared out of nowhere and smacked me in the face, nearly knocking my glasses from my nose. "Ow!"

Dagmar appeared by my side, her steps impossibly light and her expression extremely unpleasant. "This forest seems to enjoy playing with you. Perhaps because you are a weak, useless mortal who should have stayed well enough out of this!"

I ducked under the tree branch after straightening my glasses, deciding just how politic I wanted to be with Miss Grumpypants here. "Look, I get the impression that you don't much like me. That's all fine and dandy, really. I hate to break it to you, though, but you're just as human as me."

More human, maybe, but I didn't say that.

Dagmar glowered, like I'd personally insulted her family. "I have faithfully served the queen of the Unseelie Court for twenty years, now. I am a favoured servant of hers. She has taught me the way of the forest, of the plants that can kill you and the plants that can save you. She had me trained by her greatest warriors. She fed me and clothed me, caring for me beyond any other human she kept. And she would not entrust such a valuable task to anyone else!"

I exchanged a glance with Shakespeare, who flicked a single ear, then nodded at Dagmar. "Whatever you say. I wasn't aware, though, that the Fae cared that much for the mortals who hung around. Hard to care for something that gives blind obedience in exchange for some of that Fae magic."

Dagmar wrapped a hand around my throat. I hadn't even seen her move, which would have been quite impressive had I not been gagging and scrabbling for freedom. Shakespeare hissed, the sound something like a chainsaw. Dagmar's fingers wrapped tighter into my throat.

"Do not come any closer, malk," she said firmly. Shakespeare let out a growl and extended his claws. My eyes started to go blurry. To me, Dagmar said, "You know *nothing* of the Fae!"

"Wanna bet?" I squeaked. Dagmar bared her teeth, but she released me. Orders from her mistress were probably more pressing than killing me with one hand. Not that it would take, mind you. I rubbed my throat and coughed twice, just to make sure everything was working properly. My vocal cords were a little rough, but they worked. "Okay, fine. I met a girl a couple of weeks ago. She had been stolen from her life and replaced with a changeling."

Dagmar shrugged one shoulder. "It is a common practise," she sniffed. "It allows the Fae to gather energy and magic from the mortal realm. Potential is a valuable resource."

"Yeah," I nodded, "by fulfilling a *role*, a *story*. Once any potential energy is taken from the child's family by wreaking havoc and causing mayhem, basically draining that family, the Faerie comes back here."

Dagmar nodded. "Again, it is a common—"

"But what about those human children who are replaced?" I remembered Jahanara lying in her bed, dying for want of something that felt more real to her than reality. The Fae replaced her very human ability to choose with a role, a singular purpose that made everything seem more firm. Couple that with magic and the life that Jahanara had escaped felt more like the truth than anything else. Returning to the mortal realm, to a life where she *had* to choose just by virtue of being human, it was killing her.

The uncertainty and limitless potential, it had been choking her to death. That was the legacy of the Fae.

I looked at Dagmar and wondered if she were not the other side of that coin: a mortal who hadn't been returned but had grown up here, in a place where choice was a myth for mortals. Where her every purpose had been decided for her and where contemplating her own future, free of servitude, had never even occurred to her. Would being presented with a choice kill her, I wondered.

"She was dying," I explained. "The Fae had forced her into a role—servant—and made it her only purpose. They had fed her food laced with magic and they had crafted a reality in her mind that was incapable of dealing with anything else. I had to turn her into a Faerie to save her life."

Dagmar rounded on me, her hands reaching for me again. She grabbed my shoulders instead of my throat, for which I was quite grateful, and shook me. "You turned a *human* into Fae?!"

"Um, yeah," I managed. Dagmar shook me again, then released me and held up her hands, her eyes wide with unspoken apology. She paced back and forth, somehow managing to avoid all the entangling plants with her light step. Shakespeare sidled closer to me, winding his shoulders through my legs. I wasn't sure if he was showing affection or trying to trip me.

"There are hidden depths to you, Cal," Shakespeare murmured, his voice quiet enough that Dagmar, still pacing and now talking to herself, wouldn't hear. "Why didn't you tell me you'd before had dealings with the Fae?"

"Actually, I've had a couple," I said. "A fetch, banshee, and red cap in the mortal realm. Then the human half of a changeling situation...though, this is my first time trapising through Faerie."

"Who else have you gotten entangled with?" Shakespeare asked, narrowing his eyes at me. "And, for that matter, how did you survive these encounters?"

"Ah, well, that's an interesting and complicated story," I said, holding up a finger. Before I could explain, Dagmar finished her pacing and stepped close enough to me to make me uncomfortable. Her eyes were wide and looked right into mine. I pulled off my glasses and cleaned the lenses, avoiding that desperate spark of hope I saw.

"Can you do it again?" Dagmar breathed.

"Do what? Turn a human...oh, no." I shook my head vehemently. Stepping over Shakespeare and getting a good seven feet away from Dagmar, I shook my head again. "I'm not going to turn you into a Faerie!"

You'd think I'd killed her best friend from the way that Dagmar deflated before me. Her shoulders slumped and she actually scuffed her boot on the ground like a disappointed teenager. Her tattoo turned a tarnished shade of silver and I swore that I saw Grendel start to overcome Beowulf. Dagmar huffed. "It's because I yelled at you, isn't it?"

"Um, no. It's because I think it's an incredibly stupid thing to do, and because I don't actually know how to replicate the process." Actually, I had a pretty good idea how to replicate the process on *my* end, I just didn't know how to get Dagmar, or anyone, into a situation where they were ready to be turned into Fae.

"It's not stupid," Dagmar whispered, clenching her fists at her side. She straightened her shoulders and lifted her chin. In that moment, despite the fact that she was human, she reminded me a whole lot of the half-giantess, Charlotte, whom I'd watched die more than five hundred years ago. A warrior, defiant until the last. My throat tightened, though the sadness soon faded.

"Sorry," I muttered, about all the apology I could manage. "Come on, we'd better find a place to stop for the night. I don't want to be stuck out here when some nocturnal nasty decides that we're a good meal."

"I'm far more dangerous than whatever creatures are wandering around at this time of year," Shakespeare purred, rising to his feet. He was a large cat, but I had seen things in that throne room that looked like they could take him. Out here, things were likely far less civilised.

"We can stop when we reach the border with the Seelie lands," Dagmar said. "It's not far, now."

"You want to camp on Seelie lands?" Shakespeare flattened his ears. "You *are* stupid. It's one thing to be caught here, when we're already on a quest for Winter, but *there*? Far worse."

I nodded at Shakespeare. "I'm with him. If he says it's a bad idea, it's a bad idea. We can try to sneak through during the day, when we can actually see where we're going."

Dagmar frowned, making her look even more like Charlotte, and that tightness in my throat reared its ugly head again. Now was really not the best time to get sentimental. I had to get this item from the heart of Summer Fae territory and then get back to Death's lands, Mischief and Mayhem in tow, before Death finished with jury duty. I didn't have time to be taking a trip down memory lane.

"Seelie Fae are most active during the day. We won't be in nearly as much danger camping on their land as Unseelie land." Dagmar started walking off again, not waiting for us to agree with her, just assuming that we would do what she said. I would have to have a conversation with her about discussions and consensus and making healthy choices, but for now, I decided following was just easier.

"You're going to listen to her?" Shakespeare asked, falling into step beside me. His tail was puffed out to twice its size and he did not look the least bit happy.

"It makes sense," I said. "Seelie and Unseelie are generally opposites, right? So Darkness and Winter and stuff means that the others are Light and Summer and that means that daylight it probably more their thing."

"Yes," Shakespeare said, "but the fact that you are also blindly trusting that warrior woman is questionable. Faeries may not be able to lie, but they train their human servants to do so very well. I wouldn't trust her."

"I don't," I said, though for entirely different reasons than what Shakespeare was implying. "She wants to be turned into a Faerie. Probably been dreaming about how to bridge that gap since she was brought here." I watched her stalk through the forest and sighed. "I get it. It's tough being only human when you're surrounded by incredibly beautiful, powerful beings."

"Given what you've told me, I doubt that you are *only* human," Shakespeare said, sounding as though he were musing some things out, or rather fishing for information. I raised my brows at him.

"I'm not. I was talking about *her*. In any case, I now have something she wants, whether I intended it that way. She'll help us, because she wants what I can give her. So, if she says we camp on Summer court land, then that's where we camp. Or, at least, close to the border, in case a tactical retreat is necessary." I ignored the tiny growl that Shakespeare made in conjunction with the rolling of his eyes. Instead, I smacked almost face first into Dagmar's back.

I fell back onto the ground, the sludge that I had been slowly gathering on my shoes all day now on the back of my trousers and all over my hands. I scrambled to my feet and shook off the muck from my hands. "Ugh! It's like this whole place just wants to coat me in compost."

"Shut up, *Cal*," Dagmar hissed. I was tempted to ignore her and continue my complaints, but I had found that when people used that particular tone, I should listen. So I did.

We had stopped at the edge of the forest. The trees, the impossibly thick undergrowth, the tangle of ivies and migrating mushrooms—and stationary mushrooms—it all just stopped without a single trace of warning. What was left was a great wide field of grass as tall as my shin, with several small hills sticking up out of the ground, as if some burrowing creature had fallen asleep there and the land had just grown around it. Them, I should say, as there were about seven.

"Wights," Shakespeare growled, crouching low to the ground, only the tip of his tail twitching. "You brought us through wight territory."

"Wight?" I asked. "As in barrow-wight? As in Tolkien?"

Dagmar rolled her eyes, taking two steps back into the forest so we weren't right on the edge of this "wight territory". The trees closed around us as though the field of hills wasn't even there. "Barrow-wights are invention," she said. "Tolkien borrowed them from the Norse idea of vettir, dead spirits, guarding their graves. *Wights*, or Wichts, as they were earlier known, are simply sentient spirits that guard a particular area. In this case, they're a type of mist-born wraith that guard caches of treasure."

I knew a wraith; Yggdral, or Iggy as I called him, was a wraith who worked for Death as his personal chauffeur. Except for the fact that I'd never heard him say one word, and the fact that his eyes were literally balls of icy-blue fire, he was not completely terrifying. And he drove really fantastic cars.

"Oh," I said. "That's actually pretty cool."

"No," Shakespeare said, batting at me with a paw, "it's not. These treasures are things sought by beings whose very names have been forgotten. They're impossibly valuable and extremely powerful. The fact that the wights haven't been defeated means that they're *rather dangerous*. And you, idiot spawn of a porcupine, got us right into the middle of this mess."

"As long as we don't try to steal anything, it

shouldn't be a problem, right?" I was, for once, trying to be hopeful. It was a little strange, like wearing shorts in the middle of a snowstorm, and I had a feeling that sneaky cynicism was perhaps a better place to be. Especially when both Shakespeare and Dagmar exchanged a glance.

"You've never met a wraith, have you?" Shakespeare asked.

"I've met Yggdral," I said, trying not to sound superior. "He's a nice guy. Granted, he's the only wraith I've met, but still. There may be rather a lot of Elsewhere that I haven't had the chance to explore, seeing as I've been rather busy marketing for your master, not to mention doing favours for—"

Dagmar held up a hand and I stopped my tirade on how much I needed a proper vacation. Her eyes darted around as though looking for one of these wraiths to come sneaking up on us. "A mist-born wraith is a spirit that survives off the life essence and souls of those beings who still have life. If they do not consume the life essence or soul of another being, their own remaining essence will dissipate into nothingness. They are extremely capable hunters of the living and while their kills may be quick, no one said they were pleasant."

I nodded, keeping my expression serious for the benefit of my companions, who seemed actually worried—whether about my chances, or theirs, I wasn't certain. "So these mist-born wraiths survive on souls or essence, right?"

"Right," Shakespeare said. "They have an agreement with the Winter queen to keep to this part of the border and not encroach on her territory, and she sends a steady stream of vassals to try and rob the treasure, thus providing sustenance. No one ever returns from here."

"Well, then this should be just fine!" I said cheerily and marched right out of the forest and into the territory of the wights.

7

CAT SENSE

efore I could get ten feet, Shakespeare bounded up behind me and proceeded to bite me in the right ankle. I yelped and shook the cat off, throwing him a good two feet. I stared down at the now-ruined pair of trousers, revealing several large holes that were showing bloody punctures beneath.

"You'd better have all your vaccines," I snapped, glaring at Shakespeare, who was arching his back at me, teeth bared. "What was that for?!"

"You are about to walk into the lair of wights," Shakespeare said flatly. "I swore to assist you and therefore had to stop you from doing something so impossibly, species-ending stupid that I could barely comprehend it. Are you *insane*?!"

He was hissing quietly, as though he expected these wights to come up and attack him just for talking loudly, a mere few feet from the edge of the forest and their territory. I looked around, half-expecting to see these spirits approaching right then, hands extended and ready to eat us. I saw nothing but a pleasant, grassy field with knolls. That didn't mean these creatures weren't dangerous, though.

"Look, I appreciate your concern, but it's entirely unnecessary," I said. Shakespeare's ears flattened and he lashed his tail. "Seriously. I absolve you of anything to do with my death—though I do still want your assistance."

"You *are* insane," he concluded, advancing on me with malice in his gaze. I gathered that he was trying to herd me back to the forest and perceived safety.

I held up my hands but stood my ground. "Okay, let's look at this rationally. You and Dagmar are obviously highly-capable individuals, correct? You can, as it were, take care of yourself, even when crossing a field of highly-dangerous beings such as wights?"

Shakespeare said nothing, just jerked his head in a nod and continued advancing on me, a predator after prey. I stayed precisely where I was.

"Perhaps, even, all you need to get across this field without any harm is a decent distraction?" I offered. The cat's eyes narrowed, pupils shrinking to tiny slits of oblivion. He nodded again.

"Great!" I said, forcing up all the enthusiasm I could manage into my voice. I sounded like a cheerful infomercial dealer. "That solves that problem."

Before Shakespeare could react, or Dagmar could reach out and pull me back into the trees, I ran around the grimalkin and sprinted directly into the middle of the hills where the wights dwelled. Now, before you think I was being heroic and offering to sacrifice myself, generally speaking, remember that I had no soul and therefore couldn't die. I could, however, feel pain. The slice across my throat still hurt when my sweater rubbed on it. The holes in my right leg were probably bleeding like a sieve and were, in fact, quite painful. My feet were also complaining greatly from the trek through Faerie.

I felt pain. I *hated* pain. Even when my emotions were hay-wire, I disliked pain to such an extent that the planets would shatter if I could use that dislike as a weapon. It was the only thing that kept me from running off and doing potentially more stupid things for the sake of expediency. It was always there, lurking in the back of my mind, the demon that was my fear of pain. Even muted through my lack of soul, that fear was stronger than many of my emotions. Without the ability to die, if I were captured and tortured, I would feel pain endlessly. Yes, I healed when I died, but I could always experience more pain.

It was why I trained with Agravane. It was why I preferred to stay in my office and not go on adventures like the one I was currently having. It was also a really terrible excuse for not doing my best to protect people when I had the chance. Unfortunately, that ridiculous sense of other people's worth had gotten me into a lot of trouble—and a lot of deaths—over the last year or so.

None of them, though, had ever involved me actually running into the middle of a pack of predators, yelling, "Hey! Over here!"

They say you should try new things. I wouldn't recommend this, though.

I think the wights were just as shocked as I was at this level of stupidity, because it took them a few seconds to fall on the attack. As soon as I reached the middle of the collection of hills, the air got bitterly cold. Fog started coalescing around my feet and I could have sworn that it went straight for the bleeding punctures at my right ankle. I kept moving despite my steps slowing and the breath in my lungs freezing as I gasped in air.

"The queen has sent us a new snack," a voice whispered just behind me, the air tingling on my ear. I whirled left, trying to catch sight of whatever was there. Another voice, deeper and more breathy, chuckled just behind me to the other side.

"This one seems rather reckless. Not even trying to steal our riches," it said.

"Well, stealing is a bit rude, don't you think?" I asked, for once thankful for the muting of my emotions that kept the wobble out of my voice. "What sort of person would I be if I didn't at least try to bargain with you before stealing something?"

I felt the confusion in the air in the pause between words. The wights seemed to take shape in the fog, beings that looked like humans but were more bone than flesh and more wisp than shadow. Their eyes were the only things that looked familiar to me; like the wraith Yggdral, they had burning points of flame, hidden by the mist but intense all the same. They exchanged a glance and then turned their focus back to me, felt in the extreme cold.

"Bargain...?" a third wight asked. "This *is* a new tactic."

The first voice spoke again, coming from just behind me. I managed to keep from whirling around. Barely. "What could you possibly have to offer us, human?"

"What, you mean *besides* my soul? I hear that's sort of permanent, you know, and the whole point of a bargain is to make both parties happy." I held out my arms and turned around in a slow circle, catching glimpses of these wights as they gathered. There were about seven of them, which meant I had the attention of the whole pack. Good. "Actually, I don't think I'm carrying anything that you would want, unless you're keen on marketing?"

"...Marketing?" the breathy wight asked. "What is marketing?"

"Geez, you've never heard of marketing?" I asked, genuinely surprised. I thought *everyone* knew what marketing was. "It's basically getting the word out about you to people who aren't in the know. You tell people about who you are. Try to make you—or your product—interesting and intriguing so that people will either listen to what you have to say or buy something from you. You know, marketing."

The wights again exchanged a glance, though from

the tingle on the back of my neck, I gathered it was more amusement than confusion this time. "What product would we want to sell?" a new wight asked, chuckling in amusement. "We *keep* our treasure."

I shrugged. "You know, the chance to get more people out here. To try and steal from you. It's like an adventure or a challenge or something." Not that I would ever market such a thing to people; there were just some activities or services you didn't try to sell, for fear people would take you seriously. Shakespeare called me an idiot, but he had no idea the depths of idiocy that could be plunged.

Thankfully—or not, depending on what came next—the wights just laughed. The sound was like an engine through fog, barely heard and a sign of danger you couldn't yet see. I felt the wights close in, frost starting to appear on my fingers and, by the feel of it, my nose. My glasses were nearly completely fogged over and it made keeping track of these wispy creatures nearly impossible. Luckily for me, that wasn't my goal.

"You are certainly most amusing," one wight said, purring in my ear. "Far more so than our usual morsels."

I shrugged. "Yeah, well, I do try to be helpful."

"Indeed," the first wight said, speaking from mere inches in front of me. "But we have no need of marketing. We do, however, have need of sustenance."

I doubted they would wait for me to say something pithy after that ominous statement, so I just closed my eyes and waited for the pain, gritting my teeth together in anticipation. And stars above, did the pain come.

The temperature, already inducing frost-bite, plummeted even more. I tried to suck air into my suddenly non-functioning lungs, but the moisture in the air froze solid inside me. The cold in my fingers dove into my bones, spreading up through every joint and bone in my body, freezing the molecules already there and causing everything to crack, to expand and to shatter. Ice coated my eyes, blacking out my vision. I didn't die from hypothermia reaching my organs and shutting things down. I died from the pain of my body being cracked apart from the inside by ice.

Then, I came back.

I took a deep, desperate breath, the air that filled my lungs feeling warm by comparison to just about everything else. When the spots cleared from my vision, the wights were screaming in horror, scrabbling at one another as they fought to get away from me.

"Imposter," one wight hissed, tumbling back when I turned my head to look at it.

"Liar!" another cried, the sound similar to the wail of a banshee.

"*Murderer*" a third said, fleeing backwards on silent whispers of movement as I fixed it in my gaze. I just stuck my hands in my pockets—my clothes having survived my brief internment as an icicle—and hid the trembling as my body fought the memory of pain.

"Reaper," I said to the wights. As one, they hissed and vanished. The fog vanished with them, bringing back the clear evening and the calm impression of the barrows in the field. It was as if the wights had never been there, as if this place were nothing more than a pleasant meadow in the middle of an overgrown forest.

I took a deep breath in through my nose and rubbed my arms. I knew that the cold temperature was gone, that it was nothing more than the same average autumn evening that it had been before I ventured into the midst of the wights, but something in me couldn't forget the cold. It was like I had taken some of the mist-born wraith power into me, that cold lingering in the empty places that lay within, trying to get a foothold, to replace what had been lost.

Life's power within me roiled, louder than before. It was answered by Death's call, a subtle whisper that spoke of inevitability, of promise, of the end. They battled together for a moment, then tried to pull apart. I was stuck in the middle, still breathtakingly cold. So I shivered and kept shivering, even as I walked through the hills and onwards, past the mounds that hid supposedly endless treasure and terrified wights.

I could have taken some pieces, I knew, and no one would have been able to stop me, but I wasn't interested. I hadn't earned it. Besides, some things were better left hidden away. That, and I don't think that my hands would actually hold on if I tried to take something. I blew on them to try and return circulation and received only tingles in return.

I left the field behind and crossed into a patch of forest that looked remarkably similar to the forest I had left on the other side of the meadow. The trees were still old, tangled with vines. The ground was still covered in leaves and undergrowth. Even the light looked the same. But there was something indescribably different about this part of the forest, as if it were of a different personality than the one I'd left.

"Faerie is weird," I said aloud as I crossed into the woods. That statement earned me a massive thud to my right shin. I fell to the ground, barely fast enough to get my hands up and protect my face as I fell. When I turned over, there was a cat head right infront of mine. Shakespeare stood on my chest, his claws digging into my skin. He brought his head closer and, in a moment of rare and really terrifying affection, rubbed his face on my chin, while purring, too.

I was fairly certain that I was going to have a heart attack.

I lifted a hand and scratched his ear, at which point he tried to bite me. We both detached ourselves from one another and I leaned back against the trunk of a tree.

"You are not dead," Dagmar said, standing over me with her arms crossed and her expression incredulous. She had a twig and several blades of grass in her hair and her breeches were covered in mud.

"Nope," I said. "Not dead."

"Imbecile," Shakespeare spat, his brief affection gone and replaced with the haughty tone I was used to.

"Perhaps. But it's not important right now. We all made it, didn't we?," I said, bringing my arms around my middle to see about hugging some warmth back into me. The two of them continued to look at me as if I were some strange mix of crazy and myth. I sighed. "It's a very long story. We can discuss it later."

Dagmar and Shakespeare exchanged a look. I couldn't quite tell what the look meant, but I didn't think it was a good thing. Actually, I think they were having some sort of silent conversation about me. I sighed and rubbed my hands together; they had a distinctly grey look.

"Are we going to keep walking, or are we going to set up camp here? Because if we are, I want a fire," I said. Shakespeare tentatively stuck out his head and sniffed me, his ears flattening.

"He does not *appear* to be possessed by a wight," Shakespeare said. I straightened, thoughts of my grey fingers vanishing.

"Hold up, what? You didn't mention *possession* in your explanation of the dangers of the wights." I tried to take mental stock of everything. I felt fine, but that didn't really mean a lot considering my emotional and physical responses were basically null and void. I could go days without eating and not notice it—Yolanda and Agravane had explained to me, repeatedly, that this was a Bad Thing and I did my best to eat on the regular, but when you don't notice such sensations as hunger or thirst or tiredness, it's hard to do. Anyways, I felt fine and I didn't think there was someone else having a ridealong. I'd done that before, too, and could usually tell.

"It is rare, but it happens," Dagmar said. She pulled out her knife and started examining the blade, her eyes watching me for my reaction. "The wraiths can latch on to a person's soul and feed off of it, slowly, like a parasite. They influence thoughts and actions and—"

"Latch on to a person's soul?" I asked.

Dagmar nodded. Shakespeare flicked his ear in agreement.

"Oh, well, then there's no problem."

Dagmar crouched down in front of me, narrowing her eyes and extending the tip of her knife in my direction as though she intended to spear me with her knife should I give the wrong answer. You know? I was rather tired of people pointing weapons at me. "Explain," Dagmar said in a low voice that rang with barely-contained violence.

I rubbed my right eye and fought a yawn. Shakespeare started to growl, low and ferocious. I pointed at him and Dagmar. "I'm going to explain this once and then you two are going to get over yourselves. I. Have. No. Soul. There, we're done and can get on with making a fire."

Dagmar spluttered and recoiled backwards as if I'd done something completely crazy, like drawing my own knife and threatening her with it. She crawled back on her hands and actually hissed at me, like Shakespeare. The cat, for his part, just chuckled and nodded, sitting primly and wrapping his tail neatly around his paws.

"So *you're* the one," he said. I raised a questioning

eyebrow. "Death mentioned that he lost an employee's soul a while back. I initially thought he was being metaphorical, like he had exercised his will to kill someone. He assured me he was serious. Well, well, you do not look as impressive as I would have thought, but one cannot complain if the tools available are a touch rusty."

I stuck my tongue out at the Faerie cat. His words were a little like a raindrop striking you in the eye just behind your glasses.

"*Death* did this?" Dagmar asked, making some sort of sign on her chest as if to ward me off. "He made you an abomination!"

"Now that's just hurtful." I pressed a hand against my chest in mock despair, feeling once again the coldness still in my fingers. I really needed that fire. Apparently cold from wights wasn't the same sort of fatal injury as I usually dealt with. Though, it could easily have been something else and I wouldn't have known the difference.

Like I needed more problems to consider.

"You should not exist," Dagmar insisted. I sighed.

"Should not and do not are entirely different things. I *do*, in fact, exist, and there is literally nothing I can do about the fact that Death lost my soul. I'm still human—for now—and while I have some lingering side effects from my lack of soul, I am neither a demon trying to steal your soul in exchange for mine, nor someone who wants to kill indiscriminately. All I want right now, actually, is a good fire to get my fingers and toes warmed up again."

To demonstrate this fact, I started gathering twigs and things to make said fire. Shakespeare, helpful being that he is, started licking his paw and wiping it over his ear. Dagmar watched me for a few moments as I brushed debris aside on the forest floor and tried to make a pile of sticks that would turn into a nice fire. I hadn't ever done scouting as a boy—I'd been far more interested in reading books and learning the power of a good spin on a story—but I'd seen some videos online and it didn't look too difficult.

"You do not want my soul?" Dagmar asked, uncurling from her defensive posture.

"What would I do with your soul? I've had Al Capone riding along and that was just weird. Not something I shall be attempting again, thank you very much," I said, emphasising my point with a shudder.

Dagmar watched me attempt to build my fire for a few more minutes, her eyes calculating my every movement as though I would leap out and strike her at any moment. Eventually, she must have decided that, between my tattered trousers, my ruined shoes, the multiple threads hanging from my sweater, the glasses, the lack of a weapon, all of these things were exactly what they appeared to be. She tucked her knife into its sheath on her back and then crawled forwards.

"You're doing it wrong," she said. "You have to put the kindling below, like this, and then start to stack the other pieces on top."

I dutifully stepped aside and pretended to listen very enthusiastically while she made the fire. Shakespeare didn't even bother to pretend to listen. He just curled up next to the flames as soon as they were lit and went to sleep. I think that was the first time I'd ever envied a cat before.

8

WET DOG SMELL

Dagmar was wildly more prepared for taking a journey than I was. Somehow, in the small satchel that she bore, there was a collection of food that could be easily made over a fire: balls of rice and dried vegetables that could be turned into soup, a collection of jerkies, some dried fruits, even chocolate and three precious marshmallows, which could be melted over some bread. Despite glaring at me for being an idiot and not bringing my own food, she was kind enough to share. Shakespeare, when he awoke, just slipped off into the forest to hunt for his own food, which was probably a good thing.

I sat as close to the fire as I could, gnawing on some of the jerky (I didn't dare ask what sort of meat it was, but it tasted like chicken, so I found I didn't much care). Inch by inch, my limbs started warming up and the lingering cold that the wights had left me with dissipated until it was just regular cold that I held.

Finally, the warring between the two powers inside me quieted, too, as if able to relax now that I was no longer so cold.

"You know, I thought Summer's lands would be warmer," I said, swallowing the last of the jerky and holding my hands up to the fire.

"They are Faeries," Dagmar said as if that explained just about everything. I looked at her blankly. With an eye-roll, she explained. "Faeries are, above all else, beings of nature. They are bound to their natures, just as they are bound to nature. They will abide by the changing of the seasons, though the winters here will never be as extreme as they are across the border, nor will the summers there be so warm."

"Beings of nature, got it. Though, honestly, they could come up with a better means of describing themselves, considering that you've got two different meanings of 'nature' going on there. But I get it, English wasn't made for such things." In fact, English was really lacking in a good deal of descriptors for most of what I had encountered in Elsewhere. There just weren't enough words to describe how amazing something was, or how terrifying in equal measure.

"Do you know why most denizens of Elsewhere speak English?" Dagmar asked, reaching around for a stick onto which she speared a marshmallow.

"Actually, I just assumed that it was something Death did when hiring me provided a decent amount of translation. Except my assistant, Yolanda, who learned her English from a correspondence course." I didn't like to let these weird, metaphysical questions bother me. I was in marketing; wondering about the political or economic or practical reasons behind everyone speaking English was beyond me.

Dagmar turned her marshmallow, roasting it a golden brown that was even on all sides. She didn't offer me one, nor did I ask. "Elsewhere is more closely linked to your mortal realms than most people know. The beings here follow their progress with great interest."

"Ah, yes, the fascination with humans." I tried to nod sagely, but in truth, I didn't quite understand it myself. Something about their capacity for choice, or the fact that they taste really good. I'd heard both theories. "You know, you're a human, too," I said, nodding to Dagmar.

She hissed, pulling her fingers away as her marshmallow caught fire. With a petulant look, she blew out the flame and placed her marshmallow on the bread, topping it with chocolate. Technically, s'mores were meant to be made with graham crackers, but the bread would double as toast, and Dagmar's satchel was small. She watched the chocolate melt ever so slowly.

"Can you really turn someone into a Faerie?" she asked.

"It's not that simple," I replied. "The situation I was involved in had extenuating circumstances."

"Such as?"

I leaned my head back and tried to make out the stars between the branches of the trees. The foliage, even with the passing of autumn, was too thick to make anything out. I lowered my gaze and found Dagmar still watching me, waiting, desperate. "For one, I was acting as Death's proxy during that time," I started, keeping my tone neutral. "I don't know that I could have done what I did without his power flowing through me."

"But you said it yourself, you can't die. You...please, isn't there some way?" Her voice went quiet and she no longer met my gaze. I wanted to reach out and grab her hand, but I stayed where I was. The fire crackled merrily between us.

"Why are you so interested in being a Faerie?"

Dagmar shoved the makeshift s'more into her mouth and chewed slowly. I waited for her to swallow before raising my brows pointedly. She lowered her s'more sandwich. "Have you ever had that feeling that something, deep inside you, is fundamentally wrong? That you are not who you were meant to be?"

"Often," I said. Though, to be fair, I did actually have something deep inside me that was fundamentally wrong. It was barely stabilised by the tug-of-war, but it was broken. I didn't think that Dagmar was being quite so literal.

"It's like that, only I *know* I was meant to stand there, with those beings who have cared for me, given me a purpose my whole life. They're so much...more. And I'm, well, not." These last words were spoken so quietly that I doubted very much I was meant to hear. What I did hear was not surprising, though. This was what I had been warned about when treating Jahanara, a couple of weeks ago.

The Fae, being bound so firmly to a single purpose and path, felt more real, more solid and full of truth, than did just about anything else, if you'd been exposed to their magic for long enough. Dagmar, from the sounds of it, had been exposed her entire life. Except for actually turning her into a Fae, there was nothing I could do for her. I just didn't have the knowledge, or the ability.

I nodded and changed the subject.

"Okay, fine. How about you tell me, then, what it is that we're meant to be stealing from the Seelie court?" I asked, holding my hands closer to the flame.

"Indeed, I should like to know that as well." Shakespeare melted from the shadows, his eyes glowing in the dim lighting. He looked like some sort of monster come straight from the darker places of Death's realm, with his black coat barely reflecting any light and only his ears and the tips of his tail gleaming white. He stepped closer and licked his jaw with his tongue, swiping away a spot of colour that was slightly lighter than his fur coat.

Blood.

I heaved a sigh. "Do you know, it is considered rude in most cultures to sneak up on someone."

Shakespeare just blinked at me once before settling in close to my side and tucking his paws neatly beneath him. His attention narrowed on Dagmar to the point where even I noticed her shifting uncomfortably.

"Let's start somewhere small, shall we? Your queen said it was just a piece of jewellery. What *kind* of jewellery?"

Dagmar hesitated again, wiping her mouth free from chocolate with the back of her hand. "It is a pendant."

"Good." I nodded, putting on my encouraging smile. It had, in the past, served me well when trying to get clients to cooperate and reveal to me all their secrets so I could be sure to keep them out of the press. Having a good publicist was like having a lawyer in that we collected and kept secrets, only we didn't charge by the hour and were far less capable with legalese. "Does this pendant have any particular significance to your queen? Maybe some trinket her... husband? The king? Maybe he bought it for her and she lost it?"

Dagmar shook her head, folding her arms tight against her middle. She looked almost as uncomfortable about this as she did talking about why she wanted to be Fae. "No, it...it doesn't have any particular emotional significance to Her Majesty."

I frowned. Sheakespeare twitched his tail beside me. "For a servant of the Fae, you have not learned their tricks particularly well," he said. Dagmar stiffened, lifting her chin.

"I serve my queen well in all that she asks of me," she insisted. Her voice started to go dark.

"You may have accomplished her tasks according to specifications, but you are unremarkable in your speech." As if to prove his point, Shakespeare yawned, showing off his pointed teeth. I poked him in the side.

"Your speech isn't terribly remarkable yourself," I said. "You were named after—"

"Yes, I am aware of my namesake's propensity for words," the cat snapped, nearly taking off my finger before I could pull it away. "However, I should inform you that my speech patterns have changed according to modern usage. If I needed—or wanted—to wax poetical, I certainly could. It is rather a dull past time."

"Then why—"

Once again, Shakespeare interrupted me. "I was referring to a Faerie's inability to lie."

It was one of those things that people had told me about the Fae, the fact that they couldn't lie. But they always seemed to speak so normally, so like a human, that I while I had known, objectively, that they spoke the truth, a part of me had assumed they lied just as well as any human. Perhaps it was the cynic in me, or the marketing specialist, but I figured that everyone twisted reality a bit, if only to improve their image. To hear that statement, again, from Shakespeare, who had nothing to gain by it that I could discern, made the claim slightly more solid.

And then it hit me, what exactly Shakespeare was trying to say about Dagmar.

"The Fae cannot lie," I said, pointing at her. She

pulled her arms closer to herself and watched me with a wary gaze. "But you're not a Faerie. You *can* lie."

"Yes," Dagmar said slowly, carefully. "I do not understand why—"

"You've been talking around this 'pendant' thing, not outright telling me the information," I said. Beside me, Shakespeare nodded his head, though he said nothing. The important pieces had already been said. "You could easily just lie to me and tell me that it has some sort of emotional significance, or that the Seelie court stole it first, or that it's just a game they play with each other, but you won't. You won't say much of *anything*, which is suspicious."

"How is being discreet suspicious?" Dagmar challenged. I could tell, though, from the way she tilted her chin upwards that I was getting close to the truth.

"You're not just being discreet, though, you're actively blocking our ability to help you retrieve this object. We're meant to be going in there as a team, stealing this object together. If you won't tell us what it is, though, then I have to assume there's something else going on. Something that we weren't told when we made the bargain with the queen. Something that a Faerie might talk around, because they wouldn't want to be bound by the truth later on. You, who *could* lie, though, won't talk about it at all."

"Stop talking in circles!" Dagmar snapped. A twig on the fire crackled with the moisture releasing from within and sparks flew into the air.

"Why won't you talk about it?" I asked. "Why not give me some answer, even if it is a lie?"

Dagmar worried her bottom lip between her teeth, eyes flashing between Shakespeare and myself. "If I tell you about the pendant, will you stop asking questions?"

"No," I said. "I'm notoriously interested in answers."

"For an ignorant human, he does have a particular ability to gather information," Shakespeare put in, not answering one way or another whether *he* would drop the issue. I decided to ignore that particular implication.

"Then I won't tell you anything," Dagmar said. She huffed and pulled a thermal blanket out of her satchel, wrapping herself in it and rolling so that she lay with her back to the flames and to me.

"Well, what do you think about this?" I asked Shakespeare once Dagmar's shoulders settled into an even rhythm of breath. I doubted she was asleep, but I also didn't care whether or not she heard our conversation. "Why isn't she providing any information, even a lie?"

"Oh, Cal, you really do not have the abilities of a chess player, do you?" Shakespeare asked, wrapping his tail around himself and lowering his head to his paws. "Well, the Unseelie queen does. And the reason she wouldn't tell us anything was because she didn't want us to see the whole picture. The more she revealed to us, the more she would be bound by what she said. She needed us to fill in the informational gaps, provide speculation on our own so that she could put her schemes into motion without anyone the wiser, without anyone actively able to lay the blame on her. This pendant, therefore, is far more significant than some trinket that she just desires. She is sending agents, one even sworn directly to her court, against the Seelie. That is usually considered an act of war."

I studied the fire, watching the seemingly random movements of the flame as it devoured the logs that Dagmar had placed there. War. All this secrecy, this lack of information, it was because Dagmar had either been ordered to reveal nothing to me, or because she didn't want to get me involved in starting a war. Even for someone with a propensity towards blind obedience, that seemed extreme.

Not that I knew all that much about Dagmar. I could surmise, certainly, but I did not know for certain. Was she truly the human half of a changeling situation? Was she here by choice or had she grown up in forced service to the Fae? She'd said that she had known them her whole life, but it could have been because she chose to go with them as a child, or because she had been taken. Even her motivation for accompanying us on this particular heist was in question, simply because I did not trust her queen.

I could just imagine Death's reaction when he realised I had started a war between the Faerie courts when he returned from jury duty. Not to mention the fact that his dogs got loose. I doubted it would be pretty.

"If there's a war, Mischief and Mayhem aren't going to be freed, are they?" I asked Shakespeare, fairly certain that he was already asleep.

"Probably not," he said, eyes closed.

I put another log on the fire and leaned back against a tree, ready to take watch. A war. The queen of Winter wanted to start a war. And you know what? I had no intention of helping her. I started running scenarios over in my mind, knowing that ignorance and foolishness would likely be the first things that got me into trouble over this. I was not going to let those dogs rot away in the Winter court just because its mistress wanted me to start a war.

What sort of dog sitter would I be, then?

With this thought, I dozed.

Dozing quickly turned to sleep, because apparently I hadn't been getting enough sleep lately. Not that such a thing was surprising, given the fact that I had been running ragged between Life and Death's demands, dealing with proxies and djinns and taxmen. I felt like I hadn't had a chance to take a breath since Death initially lost my soul to begin with, and I wasn't wrong. I resolved, as my thoughts drifted into the incoherence of sleep, to demand a vacation.

If my sleep was incoherent, then the sounds that woke me simply defied comprehension entirely.

"Avast, ye scallywags, you trespassers and monsters! Who dares to intrude on the home and territory of we who dance in spring and repine in summer? What possible answer could you give to explain what foul spirits sent you hither and—"

"Oh, for stars' sake, *shut up!*"

This last was from Dagmar, whose voice pulled me completely from sleep. I pried my eyes open, pulled off my glasses, cleaned them, decided that I was, in fact, seeing reality and not dreaming, and then let out a pointed cough. The tableau before me froze.

Dagmar was sitting up, her black hair in the distinct disarray of sleep, a single leaf pressed to the right side of her face. She had her knife out in one hand and the other was wrapped around the throat of a being that looked like a miniature human clothed in, well, dandelion puffs and clover. This being, with oversized eyes in a purple that most certainly belonged on a flower and not in someone's eyes, had its long fingers tangled in the fur on Shakespeare's tail. The cat was bristling, hackles raised and teeth bared, but no matter how he struggled, he couldn't quite seem to rip his tail free from this creature.

"So, would anyone care to explain to me what exactly is going on here?" I asked, lifting my brows and barely refraining from folding my arms. Dagmar opened her mouth to speak, but the tiny creature's voice piped up before she could so much as take a breath.

"I am Worrywart, chief of the Thimblerig Pixies, and you have been caught trespassing on the lands of the Summer court! I know the smell of Winter when I see it and you are tainted through and through. For why else would such nefarious beings such as your-selves—humans!—travel with a grimalkin, whose blood bears the scent of Death and—"

"If you don't shut up, I will claw your face off," Shakespeare threatened. The pixie with the unfortu-nate name clamped his mouth shut and glared fiercely at Shakespeare, despite being only about half his size. I nodded, looking to Dagmar for further explanation. She just shrugged.

"Okay, Worrywart," I said, "if you're a pixie, on offi-cial business for the Summer court, then where are your wings?"

I hit a nerve. The pixie turned a vibrant shade of neon pink and I could almost see steam pouring from his ears. He started waving his little fists around, taking Shakespeare's tail with him as he did so. Shakespeare let out a warning growl; Worrywart ignored him.

"My wings are none of your business!" he finally declared.

"They are, too, if you expect us to believe that you captured us in an official capacity," Dagmar said, tight-ening her grip ever so slightly on Worrywart's throat. The pixie let out a disgruntled squeak, but eventually relented and released Shakespeare's tail. Dagmar released his throat.

"You don't play fair," Worrywart complained. "You have been captured! You should be complying with my demands, as enemy combatants and emissaries of an opposing court—"

"I don't work for Winter," I said, shrugging. Worrywart gaped at me, jaw hanging open and revealing a line of tiny sharp teeth. "Therefore, I'm not an enemy combatant. Besides, don't you have to be at war to have enemy combatants?"

I didn't mention that the queen of Winter might have wanted to start a war with Summer. I figured that would have just made our excitable pixie burst with glee. Instead, he just glowered at me and folded his arms, tapping one foot as he considered.

"What are you, then?" he demanded.

"I'm running an errand for Death," I said. It was mostly true, anyways.

"And them?" Worrywart pointed accusingly at Shakespeare and Dagmar.

"Well, the grimalkin is assisting me in my errand. Incidentally, he belongs to Death." I patted Shakespeare's head in a friendly manner and the cat had the gall to curl his lip and show his fangs to me.

"And I am his guide," Dagmar blurted, her face darkening slightly as she blushed, though her skin tone didn't reveal much. Worrywart narrowed his eyes and stared at her before turning his attention to me. He narrowed his eyes further.

Then, in a puff of dandelion fluff, he whirled on his toes and started stalking away. "Well, fine, then, but if you want to go to Summer's court, you had better come with me. You won't get in without me."

We watched the creature plough his way through the undergrowth for a moment before the three of us got to our feet and started off after the pixie. I stretched and scratched my head, wondering just how terrible my bedhead was if Dagmar looked like she had slept on the ground. I was never terribly good at this outdoorsy stuff and felt like I needed two showers and a cashmere coat to make things better.

That could have just been my very confused set of emotions speaking, though. They seemed to fixate on the strangest things in the oddest situations. For example, coffee. I should have been craving coffee quite badly. It was the one thing, no matter how much food or sleep that I got that I always felt the lack. No matter how much pain and death I could ignore, no matter how much my emotional state of being fluctuated between " angry Vulcan" and "toddler with too much sugar", coffee was one thing that I always wanted.

Yet, right then, I didn't feel any particular need for caffeine. My thoughts flowed freely from how I might put together a seasonal marketing campaign for the coffee that I was now representing, to a musing on what sort of flavoured coffee the brownie who owned the company might put out for whatever holidays Elsewhere celebrated. I then got caught up in thoughts of different roasts, different ways of dressing one's coffee and—

Okay, yep, I was definitely still right in the middle of whatever my new "normal" was and now I did actually want coffee. Badly.

"What's the deal with this guy?" I asked Shakespeare as we followed along behind the pixie. For being so tiny, he sure could move through the forest without any problem. He didn't trip over massive roots that got in his path, he didn't have to try and run to keep up with those of us who had longer legs (I.e. everybody but him). He just kept a constant distance ahead of us, as well as a constant stream of conversation that none of us followed.

"Pixies are the most mischievous of the Seelie Fae. They delight in causing small problems for people, flitting about making milk sour, tying shoelaces together, that sort of thing," Shakespeare said. "But if they do something against one of the higher Fae in their court, they often get severely punished. In this case, it looks like they took his wings."

"I guess pixies are useful to turn on other people, not so much to have in your own household," I summed up. Shakespeare nodded, a smug look on his face.

"Indeed. It is far better to be a cat," he said. "Everyone expects us to cause mischief, but we are superior enough to never be punished for it."

I rolled my eyes as loudly as I could. "Right. Sure. So Worrywart there is going to take us to their headquarters?"

"Indeed," Shakespeare said. "He wishes to regain his wings. What better way to do that than to bring prisoners? Much like the plantlings that tried to take us captive."

I definitely remembered us actually being taken captive, right after my head was nearly sliced off, but I decided to keep my mouth shut. Offending Shake-speare this early in the morning, before I'd even had my coffee, was perhaps not a good idea.

"Will their castle be the same as the Unseelie castle?" I asked.

Dagmar snorted. "You are foolish and ignorant indeed if you think that—"

"Shush," Worrywart snapped, appearing in the midst of our little conversation like a puff of air. He looked incensed, his hands clenched into fists, his face edging towards neon pink again.

I stuffed my hands neatly in my pockets and waited for the pixie to say what he had to say, hopefully within a single sentence.

"We're here," he said and whirled off, nose in the air, as if he'd heard my thoughts.

"Already?" I whispered. We'd barely been walking twenty minutes. Getting to the Winter castle had taken several hours.

Dagmar shrugged, but she looked unsettled. Shakespeare sighed and shook his head. Then, as a group, we walked into a clearing and were met with what I would politely call chaos.

9
____

CATNAPPED

I had never actively participated in one of Life's parties, but I had seen them as I was passing through. They tended to be raucous, impossibly loud, full of people drinking and dancing and doing other activities that were questionable in polite society—though I had noted the more licentious of those activities were taken behind closed doors, so Life had to be given some credit there. The parties were above and beyond anything that I'd ever seen before, simply because they were in such proximity to Life.

The court of the Seelie Fae, those that allied under the banner of Summer and Spring and whatever else associated with the Seelie, was something even beyond Life's parties. Which was both impressive and terrifying.

Beings like our pixie guide were dancing to music played by what I was fairly certain were nymphs, though I hadn't known them to be of Fae origin. There were fauns laughing uproariously with each other, a glittering dust-like substance being handed around on a leaf like some sort of drug which they happily inhaled. There were brawls of various sorts between beings that were obviously trees and things that looked more like ogres than Yolanda ever would, though I wasn't certain on the relationship between trolls and ogres. It had never seemed polite to ask.

These beings were just some of the ones that I could identify. More that I couldn't were slipping through the clearing, clothed in plant life or in nothing at all. A few of the same impossibly beautiful human-like beings—Sidhe, I think they were—that had made up the elite of the Unseelie court, were lounging around having alcohol poured down their throats, or dancing with abandon, or crawling around on the lush grass with obvious libertine intent. I gathered that this place, the centre of their power, paid less heed to the changing of the seasons than the borderlands.

Shakespeare pressed closer to me and put his ears flat against his head. "They're so...disorganised," he grumbled.

Dagmar, strangely, seemed just as put off by the revelries of the Seelie court as Shakespeare. She lifted her chin and straightened her shoulders, taking a step closer to me as well and ignoring the blatant attention that she got from many of the beings. I was fairly certain that no one at all was interested in me, for which I was mildly thankful.

It was difficult enough drawing the attention of both Life and Death.

"They are beings of light and fertility and growth," Dagmar breathed, leaning her head closer to mine. "They may be considered as more benevolent to mortals, but they are nothing quite so disciplined as Winter."

That lack of discipline would not serve them well in an eventual war, I added silently. Summer had numbers—vast numbers, if their propensity towards growth was any indication—but they would still be slaughtered.

I wondered, vaguely, what the fallout would be if a whole section of Elsewhere went to war with itself. Did it happen often? Was it as natural as the changing of the seasons back in the mortal realms? Or was it more along the lines of a cataclysmic event, such as when Death and Life had a marital spat? I hated not knowing things; it made my job so much more difficult.

I was about to lean over and ask Shakespeare some of the more relevant questions when the crowd of Faeries parted and we were suddenly presented with the comparatively calm bower of a reclining queen. She was just as striking as her Winter counterpart, with hair that was made of shining sunlight and skin that was a healthy golden-brown, freckles spattered across her nose. It was such a human thing that I almost disregarded her supernatural beauty and the way she held herself with the expectation of being adored.

There were tiny cherubs and sprites floating around the Summer queen, holding out grapes for her to taste, or fanning her with a fern. The music and partying that filled the clearing seemed to fade away, as if it existed in an entirely different sphere than this bower overflowing with flowers and the buzzing of fluffy bumblebees.

Two sides of the same coin, I figured, with overwhelming surges of life being tempered by lazy afternoons where it was wiser to sit by a pond and drink tea with a book. Just as Winter could be harsh and cruel, but also suggested fires and safety at being sheltered from the storm.

Underestimating either, I figured, would be a bad idea and I revised my thoughts on the potential outcome of this theoretical war.

"Your Majesty," Worrywart said with a sweeping bow, his clover and dandelion fluff swaying as if with a gentle summer breeze. "I have brought you these emissaries from Death, as well as their guide from our sister court, they of the cold winds and dark nights, who saw sufficient to send one of their servants to bring these emissaries to you in order to—"

"Welcome," the Summer queen said with a sweeping hand, the sound of her voice like the clanging of church bells. The sound fairly knocked Worrywart off his feet and he started blushing that ridiculous shade of pink again. "It is not often that we get emissaries from Death venturing into the heart of our territories. You more often deal with the Unseelie, which is why your lands border theirs."

I gave a polite half-bow to the queen before speaking. "Well, if it helps, I work for Life, too."

This snagged her full attention and she sat up from her reclining position, green eyes flashing at me. "Indeed? How unusual."

"Yes," Dagmar said, smiling at me through gritted teeth. "How unusual indeed."

As if I was going to reveal all of my secrets to her. My goodness, these people had very unusual expectations of mortals; they must have thought us to be complete idiots! I recalled Shakespeare's frequent insults and realised that they did, indeed, consider us to be idiots. These beings were, after all, extremely powerful and possessed of such charms and graces that they could easily lure any mere mortal to their whim.

At least, I considered, all the beings of Elsewhere seemed to underestimate me equally.

"What, then, brings you to me?" the queen asked, ignoring Dagmar completely. She flicked her eyes to Shakespeare and frowned slightly, then returned her attention to me.

"Ah, well," I said, not entirely certain how to explain that I was there to steal from her and then flee back to her rivals in order to free Mischief and

Mayhem, preferably before the end of the day, because Death might very well be done with jury duty by then.

Dagmar, helpfully, said nothing, just folding her hands behind her back where I knew she had her knife. Premature explosions of violence would be spectacularly *unhelpful* at the moment. I started talking.

"I was sent to inquire as to the price of a certain piece of jewellery," I said. This conversation felt oddly familiar, a surge of deja vu that had me pausing.

The queen shifted, her posture slightly more relaxed, now, and I saw the flash of something metal at her throat. I knew, then, why this felt familiar. I had done this before. Not standing in front of a Faerie queen on a heist quest, but demanding this particular piece of jewellery, currently wrapped around the Summer queen's neck. Only, the last time I had dealt with this pendant, I had been standing in an Italian palazzo owned by vampires, wearing clothes that made me feel like I was prancing about on a stage, with a half-giantess, a time travelling journalist, and Niccolo Machiavelli himself at my side.

The Eye of Carteria.

The Summer queen noticed my attention and replied with a sly smile, one hand reaching up to touch the item in question. "You have intriguing taste, Emissary. Do you know the history of this piece?"

I swallowed back a scornful laugh and instead said, politely, "Indeed, I do."

I was, actually, personally involved with that

history. Of course, the last time I'd had contact with the pendant, I'd sent it off with Mary, The Author, to deliver to the Library at Sazhem in order to, very explicitly, keep it out of the world. The pendant was created by some super powerful wizard-type being named Carteria, who had helped to separate the realm of Elsewhere and the mortal world. The residual effects of that meant the pendant could trap a being, lock it away and keep it separate from the world. It was a means of containment and it was beyond dangerous to use.

I'd lost my friend Charlotte to it.

The fact that the Summer queen wore it around her neck like some bauble? That was a little disturbing. What was more disturbing was that it wasn't in the Library where it belonged. I didn't know how it had gotten out, and I didn't know how to return it. Whatever had happened, this was one piece of powerful magic that most certainly did not belong in the world. I was not going to lose someone else to its machinations.

The Summer queen smirked at my apparent discomfort and I made an effort to smooth any emotion from my features. I was not quite so successful with my voice, which I could feel tightening in my throat, so I kept quiet for the moment.

"Look around, Sir Emissary," she said, nodding to the party all around us. "What do you see?"

"A stereotype of an American university frat party,"

I said frankly. This earned a snort from Shakespeare. Dagmar just looked confused.

My answer caused the queen's eyes to flash again, though I couldn't say whether she was amused or displeased at my answer. "What don't you see?" she asked, voice harder.

I looked around and shrugged. Given that my knowledge of the Fae was more or less limited to the very few things that I had been told, I was unsure as to what I was meant to be looking for. As far as I could tell, all of this was perfectly normal for a Faerie court or party.

Dagmar spoke, providing an answer that was obvious as soon as she said it. "Humans. You have no mortals here, acting as servants or otherwise."

"Well done, Winter child," the Summer queen said, her tone exactly as condescending as you would expect. Dagmar bristled, but said nothing. Smart. "My counterpart is perfectly fine with using mortals, having them supply entertainment and menial labour when she could just as easily have her people perform such tasks. I won't do such a thing."

"Why not?" I asked, since it was what she seemed to want me to ask. Okay, I asked because I wanted to know, too. I'd heard that the Summer Fae were more benevolent towards mortals, more inclined to help them, to treat them well. The fact that there weren't any here, in the heart of their power, was a bit odd.

The queen regarded Dagmar and myself with a sniff and lay back against her couch of grass and clover.

The Eye of Carteria shone at her throat, taunting me. "Mortals are...unreliable. Pliable. They bend, because they are not fixed and bound by order and duty and nature. I can expect my people to do exactly as I tell them because I am their queen and they are bound to me. I can expect that they will perform precisely as their nature intends, doing what they are meant to do. But a human? Bound by what, loyalty? They may go too far. Become creative, take *initiative* and do something that would upset the balance of things that are nature-bound. My counterpart in the Unseelie Court finds this...amusing. I find it stupid."

I held up a hand. "Just a minute. You're saying you don't trust mortals because we have the ability to choose how and what to be? Because we might get creative and do something that you don't expect?"

Dagmar shifted closer to me and I could see her hand reaching for her knife. As much as I appreciated her devotion to the orders that she was given, that would still be really unhelpful at the moment. And it would more or less prove the Summer queen's point. I decided to keep talking.

"What in the world does that have to do with the price of your necklace?" I asked. I tapped Dagmar's hand as surreptitiously as I could, shaking my head at her. I'm fairly certain that every Faerie there caught the movement, but the important thing that Dagmar caught the movement. Shakespeare, too, caught the movement and his eyes gleamed as though he wanted to shred this queen for being so insolent, so smug.

Cats. What can you do?

"Were you anyone else asking, I would determine what the necklace meant to you and determine whether or not it was worth giving up. But you are mortal and therefore impossible to pin down. Your split devotions to Death and Life both prove as much." The queen reached up again and touched the necklace, as if preparing to use its power. If she did, things would go very, very badly. Whether for her or for me, I couldn't say.

"First of all, Death hired me first to act as his marketing and public relations specialist. My agreement with Life is more of a part-time gofer gig, so I'm not sure that your notion of 'split' devotions really holds much water," I said.

"Cal," Shakespeare warned with a quiet hiss. He was looking at the Fae around us, noting that their attention no longer seemed to be focused entirely on the party.

"And secondly," I said, "I thought you Fae were fond of mortals *because* of our ability to choose and to not be bound by whatever archetypes and nature things keep you playing out the same roles season after season after season."

"You are nothing but chaos, ruining the natural balance of things," the Summer queen snapped, sitting to attention once again. She even went so far as to fold her arms and glower. "Winter may appreciate chaos, but I do not! Under normal circumstances, I would help you on your way to get you out of here as quickly as possible. These are far from normal circumstances, wouldn't you agree?"

I looked around at the party and the overgrown bower and quirked an eyebrow. "Right. I see."

"Cal," Dagmar said, tugging on my sleeve. The party was officially slowing down, now, with more and more beings coming out of their stupor and preparing themselves for attack. The thing about the growing season is that's when most people and animals alike are at their strongest. They're generally well fed, they're not combatting the cold, they're ready to take on whatever challenges come their way. Winter beings might be desperate, but Summer ones are strong.

This realisation wasn't helping, so I shoved it out of my mind.

"I would not make a deal with you, *Cal*, if Death himself stood beside you." The Summer queen glared at me and I got the distinct impression that this conversation was over. She didn't care about acting like one of those benevolent Faeries from the stories, not right now. That was more to further their nature, balance, whatever. This was personal.

So I did something particularly stupid and made it even more personal.

"No problem," I said, holding up my hands. "You don't like us because we choose every moment of every day and we're unpredictable. I get it. Actually, it's precisely the reason why you won't be able to predict me when I do *this*."

With that, I lunged forwards, crossing the last foot

or two of space between the queen and myself, wrapped my fingers around the Eye of Carteria, and pulled it off her neck. I had about a half-second before she realised what had happened and I used that time to do something that was marginally less stupid.

I ran.

10

RUNNING WITH THE DOGS

Under these same circumstances, had I been feeling or acting more normally, I would have likely just focused on running away. As it turns out, I was very good at running away—even if I were not a great runner—and did my very best to avoid conflict unless absolutely necessary. Just then, I had found it necessary.

The part I couldn't explain was where my thoughts wandered.

"When I was a kid," I yelled as I ran, the hordes of Faeries behind me, "I used to think magic was just this simple thing that you had or you didn't. Now, I'm being run down by very specific magical creatures who hate me just because I can choose what cereal to eat for breakfast. Does that sound fair to you?"

"Cal," Shakespeare yelled, running past me on paws that were far more capable than my own two feet.

"Now is really not the time for metaphysical discussions!"

"I'm turning into Yolanda," I noted aloud, with enough surprise to actually make an impression on me. I ducked as a pixie thing threw a minuscule spear at me. It hit a charging boar with two tiny Fae on its back and caused the creature to swerve off, squealing in pain.

Dagmar ran behind me, making enough noise that I tuned my head to see what she was doing and whether or not she could assist further in the effort to flee. She was assisting plenty, I decided, watching her slice her knife across a nymph made of flowers. The nymph exploded in a flash of ice and other creatures slowed as they reassessed Dagmar.

I nearly tripped over my own shoes and decided that focusing on our escape was the best course of action moving forwards. I had gotten turned around in my bid to escape and wasn't entirely sure where we had come into the clearing that housed their court. The gathering of the Summer forces to run us down was not helping my sense of direction.

"Shakespeare!" I yelled, trying to catch up to the cat, who was several lengths in front of Dagmar and myself.

"A little busy, here," he snarled, clawing viciously at a Sidhe warrior. The large, beautiful Faerie dodged the initial attack and retaliated with a large stick, perhaps the only weapon he could find in the midst of the chaos that I had caused. Shakespeare ducked and then leaped in a massive push of muscle, landing on the Faerie's face with his claws extended and his teeth ready to tear.

When the Sidhe warrior toppled a moment later, I made a point not to look at the ruination of his face. Shakespeare's bloody paws and muzzle were enough evidence for me.

"I need you to get us back to the border," I said. Shakespeare growled, but dutifully lifted his head and started scouting the area. He suddenly rounded on his paws and started running back almost the exact direction we had come. I followed him and Dagmar followed me, which meant that we three were running straight towards all the Fae that were chasing us.

As a strategy, this was not completely terrible.

The attacking Faeries hesitated as we ran headlong in their direction, possibly looking crazed, with ice twinkling on Dagmar's knife and blood on Shakespeare's claws and me just being me, the Eye of Carteria held tightly in my fist. They even went so far as to take a step backwards, uncertainty flashing over the features that I could recognise as features.

At the last possible moment, Shakespeare swerved, turning left and increasing his speed so that Dagmar and I were struggling to keep up. The Seelie were no longer quite so distracted. They had superior numbers and, despite being generally weaponless, could probably tear us to pieces if they got hold of us. I put on every burst of speed that I had and hoped that my shoes would hold together long enough to get us to the border.

We managed to make it out of the clearing without having to cause too much more damage. Shakespeare batted a pair of pixies away with his claws as if they were nothing more than toy mice. Dagmar stabbed a tree-thing in the arm with her knife and ice spread over the limb like a fungus. It let out a low scream and toppled, crashing into a good number of the party that was chasing us.

When we got into the forest, though, things became considerably more difficult. The paths that had been merely bothersome before were now treacherous. I could have sworn that I saw tree roots rise and try to trip Dagmar and myself. Shakespeare was moving fast enough that he didn't seem to get caught up in the mayhem.

I tripped twice, reaching out both times with my hands to try and stabilise myself and finding, both times, that the ferns and the ivy reached towards my hands to try and trap me. The second time, one of the more daring tendrils of ivy wrapped itself around the hand holding the Eye. I shouted in alarm and Dagmar turned, raising her knife.

"Hold still," she commanded and I seriously hoped she wasn't about to cut off my hand. It would be extremely uncomfortable and also not an immediately fatal injury, which meant that I would very much feel it and it wouldn't heal without extra help. Like, say, a surgeon to sew my limb back on.

The knife sliced past my hand with a precision that was at once both extremely relieving and had my mouth suddenly drying out. I pulled back as the ivy froze and released me, nearly stumbling into a tree whose moss-covered limbs would have wrapped around me if Dagmar hadn't grabbed my hand.

"Seriously?!" I complained, starting to run again, this time keeping pace with Dagmar in case I needed her help again. The Fae were closing in, moving through the forest as easily as if it were empty pavement. Our lead was closing, and I didn't like it.

"The queen," Dagmar said between steady breaths, "is using the forest against us, trying to trap us."

"That is so not fair," I said and yelped as an acorn whizzed past my glasses and landed on the ground with a definitive thunk.

"You are fortunate she wants that pendant back," Dagmar ground out, leaping out of the way as a maple tree lifted its root to try and tangle around her legs. Shakespeare let out a hiss up ahead and dodged a large fern spreading its fronds across the path. "If she didn't, we would hardly be able to dodge these attacks. We would be swallowed up inside a tree by now."

That sounded like a terrible idea, frankly. And I was vividly aware of the fact that things were going rather well, given the circumstances. I had literally snatched the Eye from the Summer queen's neck, right in the middle of her court and seat of power. I should have been pulled to pieces within seconds of that happening and yet we were all three running free through a forest that was under the queen's control. Yes, the forest was fighting back and yes, we still had a ways to go until we reached the border, but it was all a little suspicious.

Almost as soon as I thought it, I regretted it. In some magical situations, even *thinking* such a thing is practically invitation for something to stop you in a very definitive manner. Given that the Fae were prone towards playing out specific archetypes in accordance with their nature, a trait which I was beginning to find very annoying, my thought was most definitely the direct cause for what happened next.

I could see the border through the trees. There, just beyond the next stream, was the clearing where the wights lay in residence, a fine mist obscuring all but the largest of the barrows where they dwelt. I didn't think they would be pleased to see us again, but we would deal with the soul-eating death monsters *after* we crossed the border. We were so close.

Then, Shakespeare let out a yowl of alarm, so bone shatteringly loud that I lost all thought of running and fell flat on my face, having been tripped by a rock that appeared out of nowhere. Dagmar stumbled beside me, putting her hand out to catch herself on a tree. The bark started growing around her hand, encasing the digits in wood. Ferns and ivy started twining around my legs, pinning them to the ground. One ivy tendril tried to snake its way through the fingers of my closed fist to retrieve the Eye. I snapped at it with my teeth.

"Cal," Shakespeare said, his voice closer than I expected. "Stop."

"I'm almost free," I protested, pulling uselessly at my legs and practically dragging myself forwards to escape the plant life.

"Cal!" Dagmar said, her voice betraying her alarm. I half-expected her arm to be encased in tree bark by this point, but she was still only trapped up to the wrist. Her eyes, though, weren't focused on the tree, but on what stood before us.

I turned my head, craning my neck from my prone position and frowned. "Ah."

"Is that all you have to say?" The being who asked was female and impossibly tall, her black-as-night hair brushing the limbs of the trees. She had skin that shone as if under moonlight, despite the fact that it was barely afternoon, and what skin wasn't bare was wrapped in a long dress fitted over with leather armour. I tried to focus on her face and found myself squinting, a headache forming. She was young, impossibly so, and then she was old, wrinkles tugging at her eyes and her jowls, and then she was somewhere in between. Ravens perched on her shoulders, practically jeering.

"You're probably someone important," I said.

The woman—for I don't think she was a Faerie—smiled, showing gleaming teeth. A sword appeared in her hand and she sliced it through the air. My legs were suddenly freed. I scratched at them to try and return some of the blood flow, but I didn't try to stand.

Given the amount of sheer power that this being radiated, I doubted that standing was a good idea. No, it was far safer to sit on the ground in a nice, calm, comfortable manner.

Behind me, what sounded like a herd of poorly-coordinated elephants crashed through the growth of the forest. The Summer queen appeared, looking like a fierce hunter, a bow and arrows in her hand, a veritable hunting party behind her, mostly made up of Sidhe warriors. One of which, I noted with mild amusement, had a goodly number of scratches on his face.

The Summer queen halted at the sight of this new woman in front of us, her eyes growing wide. Without preamble, she dropped to the ground in a kneel. I blinked, revising my opinion of this newcomer's power upwards a couple of notches.

"Morrigan," the queen breathed, voice full of abject deference. "I had not expected to see you until the solstice."

This Morrigan lady, whoever she was, looked down at the Summer queen like she was barely worth noting. "I felt certain events in motion that made my early arrival seem prudent."

"So, who is she?" I whispered to Shakespeare. In response, the cat hissed in my ear, practically demanding me to be quiet. Unfortunately for him, my query had gathered attention.

"You do not know?" Morrigan asked, tilting her head. The raven on her left shoulder croaked a laugh and the one on the right buried its beak in its wing.

The Fae behind me murmured in furious whispers, likely speculating on my ignorance.

"He is nothing but a mortal," the Summer queen said with a shaky chuckle. "We cannot expect him to know the legends upon which the world was built."

Morrigan appraised me, raising a single brow in question. I shrugged.

"I am The Morrigan," she said, her voice suddenly trembling with power. "I am the threefold goddess of truth, of war, and of death. I am Elderkin, my feet having touched the earth before the Fae were born from the remains of the wars my people used to rend the world."

The trees were still shaking by the time the last word faded from the air. I considered, tried to remember my readings, and shrugged again. "An impressive introduction," I said, "but...oh, wait! I learned something about you in school. You were—are, sorry—some Celtic goddess from way back. And the Fae are primarily Celtic in background, which means...hey! You're in charge!"

"Cal, we are going to have to have a conversation about how to deal with certain beings," Shakespeare breathed in my ear, the tone sounding rather like mortification.

Morrigan, or rather The Morrigan, just laughed. "It has been some time since I have been so amused by a human, mortal or no."

"There is no question of his mortality, Morrigan," the Summer queen said with a sniff of disdain. "He and this servant that my Winter counterpart claims, mortal as the day is long."

That seemed a little rude to me, but I decided to keep my mouth shut. Dagmar, beside me, clenched her free hand and barely controlled her expression, some strong emotion, like fury, rolling through her in a tremble. The Morrigan, though, simply laughed again.

"You must reassess your perceptions of the world if you have become so blind. Or have the chains that bind you to your nature truly made you such a limited creature?" the Celtic goddess said. I wondered, precisely, what her relationship was to the Fae and whether or not she was actually in charge, as it were. I'd gathered as much given the obvious deference paid to her by the Summer queen, but that could just as easily have been from a being of slightly lesser power to one of slightly more. I didn't know enough, as usual.

That meant I had to just keep quiet and learn what I could *in situ*. Figures.

The Morrigan gestured blandly to Dagmar, still stuck in the tree, "That one is purely human, purely mortal, though she has a decidedly large amount of Fae power running through her blood, doing its best to guide her path. None of it accessible by her, I imagine."

"See?" The Summer queen lifted her chin. "Nothing with which to concern yourself."

The Morrigan ignored her. "This one," she said, pointing to me. I put a hand to my chest and tried to look innocent. "This one is far from mortal. Human, perhaps, but even that may not prevail for much longer. He has two forces warring within him, each vying for dominance. And when he decided who it is that will win, his power will be considerable."

I scowled.

"Yes," the Summer queen agreed. "I see how you could sense such a thing. He is emissary to Death, and also owes Life alleigance."

"I work for Death as his *marketing agent*. I moonlight as Life's gofer," I corrected. It was becoming rather annoying, the way people kept getting my jobs wrong. Kept assuming I was more than I was.

Reaper, my mind whispered to me, echoing through my thoughts like the untimely and unwelcome reminder that it was. I pushed the thought away, really, really not wanting to deal with the implications of that situation. Yes, I'd used the title to scare the wights away, but more than that I did not care to consider. It had been a bluff, a scare tactic, not an actual proclamation. I was perfectly happy to be human. Just human.

Frankly, compared to the denizens of Elsewhere, both mortal and immortal, magical or otherwise, being human sounded like a really fantastic gig.

"How interesting," the Morrigan said, smiling widely. "But hardly relevant, I think. Ask him. He knows, though he does not wish to know."

I was determined to keep my mouth firmly closed on such matters, but as it turns out, the Summer queen was far more concerned with other things.

"Irrelevant," she agreed with a dismissive wave of

her hand. "He has stolen from me and I demand the return of my property."

"Do not try to talk around the truth with me," the Morrigan said, the slightest hint of a sneer pulling at the corners of her mouth. "I am the truth teller, the seer, or have you forgotten?"

"The teller of truths in the day before a battle, determining who will live and who will die. Your future sight is limited," the Summer queen countered. I looked at Shakespeare, hoping for a slight clarification, but he just kept quiet, his ears twisting between speakers so that he would catch every word.

The Morrigan just shook her head, the ravens on her shoulders swaying with the movement. The one on her left shoulder cawed and flapped its wings, making enough of a rukus that the ancient Celtic goddess just brushed it from her shoulders. It flew off to land on a tree branch just above Dagmar's head, where it cawed again. Dagmar did her best to ignore it, focusing instead on pulling her hand free from the tree. She alone did not appear to be paying much attention to the conversation that we were having.

"Do you deny, then that I have a right to be here, that you are not moving directly towards a battle, the song singing in your blood just as the change of seasons moves about you?" The Morrigan took a step forwards, the sword in her hands seeming to gleam with ethereal light. If she was truly a goddess of war, then I had a pretty good idea of why she was here, and it was precisely what I had intended to stop by stealing the Eye of Carteria outright, instead of allowing Dagmar to snatch it in the name of her queen.

"You are moving towards a destruction so complete that it will tear down the very foundations upon which you and your Unseelie counterparts stand. Your natures are clashing, as ever, but here, now, there is a choice to be had. Let this mortal be moved by forces beyond his ken and start a battle that may burn you all, or call off the hunt." The Morrigan stared directly at the Summer queen, and even I felt the force of the power behind her gaze. Unbidden, I shivered, some of that wight cold returning with a vengeance.

"There's no need to go to battle on *my* account," I said with all the calm confidence that I could muster. Both parties turned their attention towards me, which was a little like looking down the barrel of two very large guns. It was very distracting and I nearly forgot what I had intended to do by speaking.

"Thief," the Summer queen hissed, taking a step closer. The ivy that had bound my feet before started growing again, reaching for the soles of my tattered shoes. "I will slit your throat and hang you upside-down from the tallest tree so that your blood may water my garden!"

I wrinkled my nose in distaste. "That sounds extreme."

"For plucking my property from my neck? From having the *gall* to touch me and violate my sanctity—" the Summer queen's words fell away, her chest heaving, as though fury itself had caused her to stop speaking.

"Whoa," I said, raising my hands, including the one holding the Eye, which I hastily lowered. "Seriously, all I did was grab the necklace."

"A petty theft, if a personal one," the Morrigan said. She raised her blade and cut away at the ivy again, the plants coiling back from the steel blade as if they couldn't stand its touch. That would be the iron thing, I figured, proving that this goddess was most definitely not Fae. Which meant her motivations in this matter were either purely motivated by telling us about this future battle, or there was something else going on.

In my experience, there was usually something else going on.

"I demand the return of my property," the queen said through gritted teeth, though she did not move forwards again.

I shook my head. "Sorry, no can do. I was told to steal the pendant and I'm literally two metres away from having completed that task, which means I can just about go home. So, no."

"Then I will kill you," the Summer queen said. I admit, I snorted.

"Good luck with that," I returned. She seemed to take this as a personal challenge, but Shakespeare had the nerve to laugh a little, drawing the attention of the Morrigan. She bent down and scratched Shakespeare's ears, getting close enough to me that I held my breath in case she wanted to test her theories about me.

"I wish to see this pendant," the Morrigan said simply.

"I can't give it to you." I tightened my grip around the Eye, feeling the edges of its octagonal design bitting into my skin, perhaps going so far as to draw blood, though I couldn't tell. I needed the pendant to get Mischief and Mayhem back. I wasn't about to hand it over to this Morrigan lady, who might want it for her own purposes.

"I did not say I wanted it, merely that I wished to see it," she said. "You have my word I shall not try to possess it."

"You should give it to me," the Summer queen snapped. Ivy and ferns alike exploded out of the ground and started dancing towards me. Dagmar let out a cry as her hand, which she had nearly chipped free form the bark of the tree, was swallowed again up to the wrist.

"Don't, Cal," Dagmar said, her breath coming in pants.

I looked between the two parties and nodded. I held out my hand towards the Morrigan and opened my fingers, which had nearly cramped shut around the pendant. There was, to my vague relief, no blood. The octagon with its minuscule inscriptions around the central crystal seemed to glow, pulsing with quiet power.

"The Eye of Carteria," the Morrigan said, sounding a bit smug, though I couldn't possibly know why. "As I suspected. Do you know what this does, young emissary?"

I curled my fingers closed again, stuffing my fist into my pocket and keeping it there. "I know enough," I said. "It captures and contains."

"In its most basic sense, yes," the Morrigan said. "It is a piece of magic so old that all but the dragons have forgotten how it works. It can contain any being, provided its bearer is strong enough to wield its chaotic potential. You know something more of that, don't you?"

I clenched my jaw and said nothing. I knew exactly what the Morrigan meant and I didn't care to discuss it. She was referring to Charlotte, the half-giantess who had been coerced into being Life's champion, forced to fight until she died. I had tried to use the Eye to contain her and save her from both Life and Death, but had ultimately not been strong enough. She had died anyways. She had been my friend and I couldn't save her.

"Then you should also know that it cannot be possessed, for it is a means of separation, of containment, not of slavery," the Morrigan said, as though she were just listing another of its traits that I had already experienced, had already known. And while I had never thought of the Eye as a means of slavery, for one being to control another, I had also not had that spelled out for me so blatantly.

A light went off in my head, probably several minutes too late. So sue me for needing things spelled out sometimes. I was a marketing agent, not a master chess player. Actually, I was, all around, terrible at chess.

I pulled the Eye out of my pocket and uncurled my fingers, which were already doing their best to lock in place around the pendant. Then, with that hand trembling and the other nearly trembling, I fished the chain out of the pendant's loop. I held it up and, with as much force as I could muster (admittedly, not much, as I was moving headlong towards exhaustion), I threw the chain at the Summer queen.

"Your property," I said with a grin.

The Faerie screamed, her voice causing the forest to shrink away from her wrath. The ivy that had tried to capture me again withered. The bark holding Dagmar in place cracked and her hand was freed. She rose to her feet with seemingly effortless movements, looped her arm through mine, and half dragged me across the border and into the territory of the wights, Shakespeare following close behind.

11

DOG WHISPERER

The Morrigan followed us across the border and witnessed me lying flat on my back where Dagmar had dropped me, staring up at the sky with a definitive scowl. Judging by the way her brows winged upwards as she caught sight of my expression, it was a very significant scowl.

"I dislike being manipulated," I said. I pushed myself into a sitting position and glared towards the border, where a few of the Seelie Fae were still lingering, probably under orders to disembowel me for catching their queen in a half-truth. The Summer queen's twisted truth was enough to make the Winter queen's words questionable as well. Then, I shifted my glare to the Morrigan herself.

"I can understand that," she said, giving me a knowing nod, the powerful goddess condescending to sympathise with the poor human.

"It's not that I'm not grateful for your help in

sussing out the truth," I said, and she took a swift breath, obviously not prepared for my attacking her, "but I really don't like being manipulated. Why did you help us?"

"I am the goddess of battle, of foresight and death. I have a perfect right to appear where a battle is about to take place," the Morrigan said, her words slow and deliberate, like she was choosing them from a list of bad options. I resisted the urge to turn my scowl into an outright look of disdain.

"I've had plenty of battles in my life, why did you choose to appear at *that* one?"

"You ask a great many questions," the Morrigan said. She spotted Shakespeare and Dagmar in the long grass, staying closer to me than was probably strictly necessary due to the creeping mist that was growing at our backs. The wights were approaching, but either because of the Morrigan or myself, they were approaching slowly. I gathered we had a few minutes, still, before we were in danger. As much as I'd like to rest, there was no use wasting the time I had.

"You have no idea," I said. "I doubt this situation had anything to do with me. You can insinuate all you like about my 'no longer mortal and who knows how human' status, but I doubt very much I'm worth your notice."

The Morrigan took another breath, this one deeper. She sighed and sheathed her sword in the sheath at the waist of her battle dress. Finally. Some answers.

"No, you are not," she said. "While interesting, as I haven't seen one of your kind in centuries, Death's creatures were never my domain. My domain is over those who are about to die, who fight in battle, and those who seek truth.."

"So, what, you were there for Dagmar?" I asked. Beside me, Dagmar stiffened. I would have sworn that I could hear her interest in her bated breath.

"No." The Morrigan shrugged a shoulder. "A warrior, she may be. Perhaps she will even die in battle. But she is not one of mine. I have no need to be present for her. Nor you, grimalkin, as cats have always held their own council."

Shakespeare flicked his ear with a superior look. "Cats have always been wise enough to know our superiority."

I stifled a cough.

"I came for them," the Morrigan said, nodding her head towards the Summer forest. The Fae that lingered there had since melted into the shadows, perhaps realising that we weren't coming back. Or perhaps they were more worried about the wights, which were getting closer. "While not truly those for whom I am responsible, they are a part of my people."

Celtic background. I understood that much, though I imagined there were far more complicated threads running between the Morrigan and the Fae. "They want to war," I said. "The Winter queen all but dangled it in front of us when she sent Dagmar along."

Dagmar hissed something rude in my ear. I ignored

her; she had surely heard Shakespeare and myself the night before, speculating as much. This shouldn't have come as a shock to her.

"And the Summer queen would have been justified in such an act had you not returned her property," the Morrigan agreed. "It is good that you are not as oblivious as some mortals."

I didn't point out that she had very nearly dangled the answer before my face. I would take the compliment to my intelligence however I could get it. "Why would a goddess of death and war and such be so worried about a war between the Fae courts?"

The Morrigan's eyes darkened and I could practically taste the power that she gathered to her. "You are capable, human, but there are some things even beyond your ken. Stick to your task. Worry about your work for Life and for Death. Leave the higher politics to those better suited to them. Or you run the risk of being manipulated, again."

Then, as easily as she'd appeared before us in the forest, she was gone. The mist that had been approaching all throughout our conversation hesitated before swirling forwards as if unimpeded. I felt my scowl returning to my features.

"I hate it when people do that," I complained. Shakespeare shrugged.

"Surely you can't expect people to tell you everything, just because you ask," he said, rising to his paws. He regarded the mist almost cavalierly, as if it not longer posed a threat, though I knew full well that the wights it concealed would be happy to become bothersome.

"It would be nice, actually," I said. I sighed and shrugged. I would just have to do some digging to find out on my own. Of course, I had several other problems facing me just then. First and foremost of which was that the mist had almost reached us. Dagmar and I stood, Dagmar pulling out her knife and slipping into a defensive stance, me putting my hands into my pockets and debating silently whether it would offend the wights if I slouched in their presence.

They surrounded us with mist before taking form, and even that form was less solid than it had been during our last encounter. They also hung back warily, as if getting too close to me would have been highly problematic. I wasn't going to complain about their caution. It made everything that much easier.

"Why do you return, Reaper?" a wight hissed, the voice somehow familiar in its rasping nature. "Have you not done enough harm?"

"If I remember correctly, you were the ones who attacked me," I said. The wights rumbled at that, the sound somewhere between a rainstorm and a cat throwing up a hairball. Shakespeare flicked his ears, as if sensing my unkind thought. I did my best to ignore him, though the direct stare of a cat, especially a Faerie cat, is quite uncomfortable.

"Yet you killed one of our own," the wight said. The others murmured agreement and swirled both closer and farther away, apparently trying to see if they could press their luck.

"Killed...?" I frowned; I remember distinctly that they were the ones trying to kill me, that I had be left to endure that seemingly endless cold that seeped into my bones. "I didn't—"

The wight who was speaking surged forwards until it was inches away from my face, though it didn't try to touch me. I could see, quite clearly, the pointed teeth, the fire-point eyes, the remains of a soul now trapped and meant to consume others just for survival. It was not an existence I would have wanted, but what did I know about that sort of life?

The wight bared its teeth at me, then retreated to a safe distance. "What do you think you are, Reaper? A benevolent creature, freeing souls from their torment? Do you delight in stealing from us the only existence that we've ever known?"

I realised, then, what it was that the wight implied. These beings were pure soul, pure essence, the very lifeblood of any living being, magical or otherwise. By touching me, I had done was it was that Reapers were meant to do; I had released a soul into whatever lies beyond Death's domain. The wights had tried to kill me and I had inadvertently killed one of their own.

I held up my hands in apology, then hurriedly put them into my pockets. It might not be the best idea to wave my threatening appendages before the very creatures who feared them.

"I'm sorry," I said, hunching my shoulders.

"Cal," Dagmar hissed, seemingly shocked by my statement. Shakespeare pressed close to my leg, whether in support or as a means to communicate his anger, I didn't know. He said nothing, just stood there. Dagmar put a hand on my shoulder, squeezing hard. I shrugged her off.

"No, really, I'm sorry," I said to the wight. It flickered before me, uncertainty playing across what few distinctive features it had. "I didn't know that my touch would...would kill you." Even if it wasn't truly death, they would not see it that way. "This is fairly new to me and...I don't have the control that I would like."

The wight hissed and moved backwards, others gathering close as if preparing to attack, or to run. They whispered amongst themselves, that rasping sound the only thing that we could hear through the thickness of the mist.

"You...are a strange Reaper," the wight said at last, floating towards the three of us. I felt Dagmar tense behind me and even Shakespeare's tail lashed against my leg. They weren't standing beside me to support me; they were standing beside me for my *protection*. If that wasn't weird enough to warrant an emotional response—one of confusion—then I didn't know what was.

"It is because he does not yet know the extent of his abilities," another wight chimed in, pressing close to the first for probably precisely the same reason Dagmar and Shakespeare pressed close to me. "He will still kill us!"

I lifted one hand in a placating gesture, making sure not to move either forwards or backwards as I lifted my palm. "I cannot promise that I will not be called here in the future," I said, wishing beyond emotion that I could make such a promise, that I could know how to refuse this change, to never become a Reaper in full, "but I can promise that I will not make any motions to hurt you without advance warning. Will that...Is that sufficient enough for a truce?"

The wights whispered amongst themselves again, darting back and forth, the mist thickening and thinning with their movements. The first wight floated forwards, and I could have sworn that I saw an almost-human face appear in its shadowy features. It, too, held out a hand and then bowed.

"A truce. In exchange for fair warning," the wight said. "You have our word."

"And you, mine." I lowered my hand and the wights vanished into the mist, which dissipated a few moments later.

Dagmar sagged against my back. For a brief moment, I wondered if she would go so far as to thank me, but instead she shoved against me with all her strength, which was considerable. I stumbled backwards, then fell flat on my back. Again.

"You are *insane!*" Dagmar snarled, lunging towards me. She pinned me down with her knee and drew her knife. "Tell me why I shouldn't take my satisfaction out on you, now."

I gave a weak, half-smile. The rest of me was trying

desperately not to heave a sigh and roll my eyes. Now, after all the fighting and the negotiating and the conversations with goddesses, Dagmar chose to throw a tantrum. I could practically see the fury sparking in her eyes, clashing with her stoic warrior persona.

"My goodness, you'd think that someone had superseded your authority," Shakespeare purred, waltzing into my line of sight with a smug look on his face that only a cat could pull off.

I looked back at Dagmar, whose mouth had straightened to a thin line. "Is *that* what you're complaining about? That I didn't follow your lead back with the Summer queen? That I snatched the Eye from off her neck without so much as a by your leave?"

"This was *my* mission! *My* task!" Dagmar thumped her chest with her hand, the other hand holding her knife with ever-whitening knuckles. I decided to lay precisely where I was and not put up a fight. Only bad things could come from angering her more.

"Then we two came and messed everything up?" I surmised. Shakespeare snickered from somewhere near my left ear.

"Surely, dear mortal, you could not expect your queen to pass up such an opportunity?" Shakespeare taunted. And he was definitely taunting, every tone on every word designed to infuriate Dagmar. "Two agents of Death, walking straight into your queen's court, offering to pay a boon in return for the release of two ridiculous *dogs*. Did you expect her to do nothing? Surely, you know she has a future to plan for and must take every, ah, *opportunity*, as it comes." Shakespeare flicked his eyes to me for a brief moment before putting on his best smugface for Dagmar.

I couldn't tell if he was trying to goad her into revealing something, or if he was just curious to see what she would do. I hoped he stopped before she tried to kill me.

Dagmar swiped her knife at the cat, who retreated with a chuckle. She remained kneeling on my chest, effectively preventing me from moving. "There were a thousand things she could have demanded of you, and yet she had to give you *my* task! After all I've done, after everything that I've sacrificed so that I could serve her, I am thrown aside as though I am worth nothing more than—"

She cut off with a harsh intake of breath, looking at me as though she had revealed something absolutely critical. In a way, she had; I understood her better than I ever had before.

I kept my voice gentle as I spoke to her, trying to use my "reasonable marketing agent" voice so that she wouldn't bite my head off for putting the puzzle pieces together. "You don't want to be just another human to her. As a species, we are considered special, interesting, dangerous, but as an individual? Practically raised in the Unseelie court, where even the lowliest plantling has more raw power than you? That puts you at the bottom of the food chain."

"Shut up," Dagmar snapped. She leaned forwards, her weight crushing my ribs. Her knife was at my throat and I would not have been surprised had that lovely line of scabbing from my encounter with the plantlings the day before been redrawn, despite being cleared away by my not-quite death.

I kept talking. "That's why you were so desperate to have me turn you into a Faerie. You wanted to be anything but human so that you could appease *her*."

"No," Dagmar insisted. She blinked rapidly and looked at me with pure murder in her eyes, for making her cry. "I am a prized servant! I have done everything my queen asked, without question or hesitation. She values me, so much more than the others."

"Ah," I said, nodding and wincing as the movement caused the knife's edge to bite farther into my neck. "You just don't want to be an *insignificant* human."

She reminded me ever more of Charlotte, just then. The half-giantess had been ostracised by her giant family, and feared by her human brethren. She had done everything in her power to prove, to herself or the world, that she was perfectly capable, even magnificent. Dagmar was equally determined to be magnificent, only her fear of the alternative kept her in complete servitude to a creature I was certain did not care for her at all.

"Enough," Shakespeare said, once again appearing in my line of sight. He put a paw out and touched Dagmar's hand gently. She flinched and pulled the knife back. "Determine your personal worth at a later date. We do have to still get back to the Winter court today."

Dagmar, with a shove that squeezed out every particle of air in my lungs, stood and strode away from my prone form, already sheathing her knife at her back. I rolled onto my knees and took in several deep breaths, ignoring Shakespeare's eye roll as I did. Then, I too stood, and we trouped off towards the path that would lead us back to the Winter court.

I was really getting tired of all this hiking. Next time I did a favour or a job or whatever for Death—or Life—I was going to wear proper hiking boots. And pack a rucksack with extra supplies. Including a phone charger; my phone was woefully close to an empty battery and I didn't want to check and see if Death had sent me any messages regarding his beloved pets.

I really hoped that Mischief and Mayhem were doing alright.

Shakespeare, in true cat fashion, seemed to know the direction of my thoughts as soon as they crossed my mind. He settled in to walk beside me, leaping lightly from tree root to boulder to the ground as we moved around and across obstacles in our path.

"I wouldn't wory too greatly about those dogs," Shakespeare said, flicking his paw with disdain as some water from the surrounding leaves dripped on it.

"Oh?" I asked, nearly tripping into a puddle almost completely obscured by ivy. "I was given explicit instructions on how to care for them and instead have left them in the care of the Winter queen. Excuse me if I don't remember that being on the list of approved care techniques."

Shakespeare snorted. "The queen is not a fool. She may be conniving and dangerous and very prone to killing, but even she is incapable of facing down Death's wrath. I imagine those two have had an easier time of things than we have, what with *your* particular ability to gather trouble."

"Me?! I haven't done *anything* to gather trouble," I said indignantly. "I have literally just been following you and Dagmar on this path, the entire time. And before you bring up what happened with the Summer queen, need I remind you that if I did not act as I did, then there would be war between the two sides of Fae?"

Shakespeare sighed melodramatically. "Hail, the conquering hero," he said drily. Then, "I have been around for a long time, Cal, and I will be around for a long time more. I have never, in all my time, seen anyone fall into as many difficult circumstances as you. It's almost like someone is deliberately getting in your way, and as there is no one else around, I have to assume that this someone is you."

I frowned at that. Indeed, this whole quest thing had seemed to be a bit...much. It was almost like someone was trying to write me into a story, trying to make sure tha tmy path on this quest followed pre-prescribed roles and guidelines. The initial trek to the border, meant to show my determination. The first encounter with the wights, a small fight to determine how capable I was in a potentially deadly situation. The helpful guide at the border of Seelie lands, both reluctant and eager to lead me directly to my quarry. The theft, my prize laying right out in the open on the Summer queen's neck. The fact that the three of us escaped the subsequent chase without so much as a permanent scratch. The appearance of the Morrigan. The negotiation and truce with the wights. Now, we were on our return journey, precisely how one would describe the conquering heros.

It was exactly how I would expect a story to play out.

I nearly stumbled again as I worked the problem through my brain and came to the only conclusion possibly available. I clamped my mouth shut so I wouldn't say anything out loud and even Shakespeare eyed me warily as I struggled to regain my balance.

Because, let's face it: *I had been played.*

This whole thing was designed to keep me moving from task to task without any real time to think. Any real time to wonder, precisely, it was that I was sent after the Eye of Carteria to begin with. Why I was encountering something that I had personally sent off to be locked away until the end of time.

The Fae, so close to war, so desperate for some hapless servant to step in and stop it—all of this was a distraction.

I reached into my pocket and wrapped my fist around the Eye, trying to wrack my brain and determine what particular property of this tiny amulet would demand that much manipulation. Or, perhaps, it wasn't the Eye at all that required manipulation, but me.

What would require the Fae—for who else could it be—to go to so much trouble over *me*?

I didn't have the answer right then, but it didn't matter. The next stage in this grand play was upon us in the form of an armed, and furious, escort of Sidhe and ogres, ready to march us back to the Winter queen like prisoners.

Goodie.

12

CRAZY AS A CAT

It turns out that there are some benefits to being marched through a forest in the wake of several ogres; they are quite easy to follow. The path, which had destroyed my shoes the day before, and which had been trying to trip me up, was widened and made easier to follow simply by virtue of being trampled down by large, unhappy-looking beings.

Ogres were, as near as I could figure, the Fae version of trolls, or perhaps it was just rock trolls that were a separate species. In any case, these beings were at least a head taller than Yolanda—an impressive feat —but were hunched over by their massive slabs of muscle in their back and shoulders and looked, therefore, like they were shorter than she was. Their arms dragged near their knees and they trudged with all the grace of cows.

No offence to cows.

The Sidhe warriors, by comparison, were like

dancers. They were beautiful and dangerous and absolutely did not let Dagmar, Shakespeare or myself get close enough to each other to have a conversation. I couldn't relay my theories about being manipulated and I couldn't discern what it was that Dagmar was thinking.

Because, my goodness, was she thinking.

Her steps were light and measured, walking in the ogres' path like it was something that she had been doing her whole life. She kept her hands relaxed at her side, but I saw her eyeing the Sidhe out of the corner of her eye as they moved past, sometimes darting in to say something—likely derogatory, given their gleeful laughter—to her and then dart away again. Dagmar's expression deepened as we walked on, falling into a mask of absolute calm. It was a mask designed to never let anyone know what you were thinking. I imagined that she'd perfected that mask over her lifetime in the Faerie courts. She was definitely mulling something over, and I wanted to know what.

Shakespeare sauntered along as though this whole thing was a procession done in his honour. His tail was held at a jaunty angle and his ears swivelled around as he listened to the Sidhe and the ogres. Not once did he glance at me, but I would occasionally see an ear twitch in my direction. A mild reassurance.

None of the ogres or the Sidhe bothered to talk with me. They kept me in my appointed walking position, but ventured no closer. I couldn't tell that they were even that bothered about me, given how uninterested they seemed in me.

Frankly, I was okay with the peace. It gave me more time to try and puzzle out just what was going on.

I could come up with absolutely no reason why the Fae would be interested in manipulating me. They surely had to know about me, even cursorily, before I waltzed into their territory, simply by virtue of the fact that I was Death's marketing agent and I had my various social media pages and was in contact with creatures from all over Elsewhere. I had also interacted with some of their mortal number not too long ago, when I sorted out the whole back taxes situation. Then there was Jahanara, whom I had turned into a Fae.

Was that it? Did they want to test me, to see if I posed a danger to them because I had once turned a human into a Fae? Did they want to use me? Perhaps that was why Dagmar had been sent along; she desperately wanted to be anything other than human and had latched onto the hope I could provide that dream to her.

I couldn't.

I think.

But did the Fae know that? Could that have been the reason?

It was a possibility, I decided. I fingered the Eye in my pocket and felt the now-familiar etchings around its edges. It was definitely a possibility, but there were holes. The Eye was just the biggest one.

What in the world would the Fae, of either side,

want with the Eye of Carteria. Who did they want to contain? It was an impossibly strong magical amulet and using it required a very precise amount of control and intent. What had the Morrigan said? That it took much to control it's chaotic potential. Potential, it would seem, was not something the Fae were good at, if they disliked even the potential of mortals so much.

Potential. I blinked, faltering in my steps enough that the whole party turned to glare at me. I gave a weak smile and tried really hard not to think about the amulet in my pocket.

After what felt like far too long, we arrived back at the seat of the Winter queen. The castle was exactly like we had left it. The throne room even seemed to hold the same people, dressed in the same clothes— though I saw a slight shift in colour to something darker, more earthy. As before, the courtiers parted before us, their expressions a mixture of arrogance, dislike and interest, as the three of us walked past.

The ogres broke off about half-way through the parade of people, apparently no longer needed. The Sidhe warriors escorted us the entire way to the throne and then bowed deeply before the Winter queen. She lounged on the throne with her legs thrown over the arms in a posture that was at once casual and calculating. She watched the three of us with a veiled expression, her finger tracing snowflakes on the stone of her throne.

At the base of the throne lay Mischief and Mayhem.

They looked miserable.

Mischief raised her head slightly when I approached and I saw the tip of Mayhem's tail wag. The queen shuffled and the two dogs winced, their ears going back.

I was instantly furious.

The sensation came out of nowhere, like a tornado on a bright day in the middle of Kansas. I'd once watched a documentary showing the absolute destruction of the massive cyclone, coming out of a seemingly calm day and leaving chaos in its wake. This fury was like that.

"You *swore* they would be taken care of," I snarled at the Winter queen. She blinked and sat up straight, regarding me with a quirked brow.

"I see you have returned in one piece," she commented. "And you are not trailing Seelie Fae in your wake, so I gather your task was unsuccessful. How terribly interesting."

I dug into my pocket and pulled out the Eye of Carteria, flashing it for everyone around to see. The queen sucked in a breath and her gaze shifted to Dagmar, who stood tall, chin raised. The queen looked back at me.

"Well, well, how very unexpected. It would appear that Death has chosen a capable—"

"You *swore* that you would look after Mischief and Mayhem," I said again. Mischief whined from where she sat on the dias. I put the Eye back into my pocket, very deliberately, and waited for the queen to answer for her crimes. The queen smiled a look of complete satisfaction and leaned back in her throne, completely at ease.

"I swore no such thing," she purred.

"You swore safe—"

"Passage, dear Cal," the queen interrupted. I clenched my fist, but realised that she was right. She had not sworn to see to the needs of Mischief and Mayhem in my absense. She had simply implied. And Shakespeare seemed to think it was alright.

I looked at the grimalkin, now, and could not tell whether he was shocked by his companions' treatment or if he were unsurprised. He just sat there, his tail wrapped around his paws, only the white tip twitching.

"Come here, Mischief, Mayhem," I said, tempering my voice so that the anger running through it didn't sound completely overwhelming. Mischief did not hesitate. She scrambled off the dais and ran to me, her tail tucked between her legs and her ears flat. Mayhem followed, slower, his steps careful and his eyes wide.

"They took the ball," he said softly, thrusting his head into my hip, as if I could provide the protection they couldn't manage on their own.

"I'll buy you ten more," I promised. Just to be sure he knew how serious I was, I promised it to him twice more, binding me in Fae style. He gave the barest hint of a tail wag at that. "You're both such good dogs," I said, scratching their ears. "Now, take Shakespeare and go home. Okay?"

"Okay," Mischief whispered. She licked my fingers

and then slunk through the court. Mayhem nosed Shakespeare in the side to move the cat along. Shakespeare hissed.

"I would remain," he said. Mayhem looked at me.

"No." I pointed after Mischief. "You swore to assist in retrieving Mischief and Mayhem. I will only consider that bargain complete if you return home with them *now*."

Shakespeare stood, arching his back and showing off his size. His claws extended, raking into the stone floor. The fur on his back rose into the air. I just pointed after Mischief and said, "Now."

With a disgusted snort, Shakespeare trotted after the dog, Mayhem taking up the rear. I waited until all three were safely away before turning my attention back to the queen. They had safe passage and would likely not get into any trouble, now that they were free of the court.

"Very well, Cal," the Winter queen said, tracing a finger back and forth on the arm of her throne, icicles forming in her wake, as though she were simply bored with the whole proceedings. "I have fulfilled my bargain. It is time you fulfilled yours."

I pulled out the Eye and held it up again, pretending to admire the pendant. Then, with all the disdain I could muster, I sneered at the queen. "I already have."

The temperature dropped several degrees. The throne beneath the Winter queen squealed as if the sudden cold would crack it into pieces. She leaned forwards, staring at me. "What did you say?"

"I swore I would, let's see, *retrieve* a particular piece of jewellery from the Seelie. Well, to my mind, I have done just that. I retrieved it. You never said I had to deliver it to your hand. You never said I had to give it to you. You simply said *retrieve*." I held the pendant up and smiled brightly before putting it back into my pocket.

The queen roared her wrath, rising to her feet with the swiftness of a winter storm. She strode off the dais, marching towards me with the intent to kill plain in her eyes. I held up a finger, halting her in her path.

"Ah, ah," I warned. "I was promised safe passage. I haven't yet returned to Death's lands, so you are still bound."

The queen snarled wordlessly, ice lashing out at various courtiers, as if they were the only possible targets for her fury, since I had taken that from her. I decided that I might as well push my luck. I kept talking.

"See, here's the thing. You sent me along to the Summer court with a very particular outcome in mind. You *wanted* to go to war with the Seelie. You *wanted* Dagmar here to retrieve the necklace. An agent of the Unseelie, acting in direct opposition to the Seelie, it would have been an act impossible to ignore. An act of war. The fact that your agent was human would have meant nothing. The fact that she was working in accordance with me, an emissary of Death, would have meant nothing. She could have been acting all on her own and you still would have been drawn into war."

I stepped out of the way of the queen and walked towards Dagmar. I rested my hand on her shoulder and she stiffened.

"The Seelie would have blamed you. The Unseelie would have denied you were acting on their orders. Righteous fury on one side, with indignant offence on the other. The perfect storm. And I would have helped precipitate the whole thing. The question, though, is *why*?"

Silence filled the air. The particles of ice and snow that were floating about followed my every movement, but did not attack. Wounded courtiers glared in anger, but did not move from where they stood. Dagmar kept her jaw stiff and said nothing.

I smiled. Squeezed Dagmar's shoulder. Then, I kept talking.

"Why in the world would the two courts of Fae want to go to war against each other?" I mused. "Now, granted, I don't know a whole lot about Fae. The ones I experienced in the mortal realms were obviously your far weaker denizens. Predators amongst mortals, but weak fodder for sport here. Isn't that how it works? In any case, what little I do know about the Fae indicates that you are working in balance. You represent one side of the coin and they represent the other. You work in accordance with your natures, and with Nature herself. As with Life and Death, too, as it turns out.

Those both demand balance, no? War is anything but balance."

Even as I spoke of the forced of Life and Death, I could feel their opposing powers inside me, pulling me apart and keeping me together. It was like an itch that you could ignore until you actually thought about it. I took a deep breath.

The queen tightened her hands into fists, but said nothing, her eyes following me as though preparing to pounce. I stepped up the dais and walked around the throne like a tourist admiring a piece of architecture.

"A war, then, would prove impossible. Perhaps inevitable, given how often you and your counterparts' natures clash, but also impossible. Because the thing about war is that it may start with two opposing sides, but what often remains is nothing more than chaos. No balance. No natures to obey. Just chaos. My two employers are the exception to this rule, I think, given that their very beings are chaotic. So, what, you two sides are left with no recourse but to keep hating one another? Working to undo all the other side's hard work, but with no real way to fight and win. What a depressing existence."

I circled around to the front of the throne again and, perhaps that same tornado of fury demanding that I do something to enrage them, to foce the queen to act against her bargain, I sat. The stone was cold, like going out in a blizzard quite naked. My skin protested and my breath came out in a puff of air. I wrinkled my nose.

Someone, Dagmar I think, gasped in horror at what I had done. I reached into my pocket and, once again pulled out the Eye. I held it up to the light streaming in from the stained glass windows, watching the patterns created by the blue stone in the centre dance across the frozen ground.

"Pretty little thing, this," I said. "Quite old, too. At least, it was old the last time I saw it, and that was several centuries ago."

"You *know* this amulet?" the Winter queen breathed, alarm creeping across her features for the first time. I smiled wanly and nodded.

"Oh, yes. I was the one who sent it to the Library at Sazhem to begin with," I said flatly. "So I know exactly what it does. I know that it requires strength and focus to capture its potential. I even know how to use it."

I didn't add that while I had tried to wield it before, it hadn't gone well. Still, my admission gathered the exact attention that I had hoped. The Winter queen and her courtiers, those from Autumn or Darkness or Cold, all fixed their attention on me with bated breath, a slight sliver of hope ringing through the coldness. I tucked the amulet back into my pocket and leaned back on the throne.

"You could use it," the queen said, stepping closer, her expression eager. She licked her lips.

"Oh, indeed. I could do exactly what you want. I could go and trap the Summer queen. I could tip the balance. I could do what you sent Dagmar to do—the only human amongst you and therefore the only one who could act against the balance, the only one who could actually *use* the amulet, because she still has choice and therefore can command potential. That was why you needed a mortal, why you kept her around all these years. And in return, what, you would finally make her Fae? Is that where I come in?"

I rose from the throne, wondering vaguely if I left pieces of my clothes seared to the cold stone as I did. Almost immediately upon rising, though, blood began to flow back into my extremities and my bum began to tingle with renewed feeling. A most uncomfortable sensation, mind.

I walked up to the Winter queen, now standing at the base of the dais, her face upturned towards mine. I leaned close, smiling. She smiled in return, elation playing across her features.

"It's not going to happen," I breathed. Then, I strode down the dais and walked towards the door. The Fae could go rot in the tropics for all I cared. I really, really hated being manipulated.

I heard a scream of rage behind me and the wind whipped up to exponential proportions. Where before, the courtiers were keeping still, watching all of this play out like it was some grand, highly-entertaining game, now they fled, scrambling towards whatever door led to another part of the castle, or even moving towards the exit. I kept moving at an even pace, knowing full well that none of them could touch me without breaking the Winter queen's bargain. Even if they did, it would not do lasting damage.

Then, there was another scream. This one was human.

I turned, facing the carnage that I had left in my wake.

Several of the Fae courtiers were stumbling away, gravely wounded. None of them were dead. Dying, perhaps, but not immediately. The rest of the room was remarkably clear, given how many had packed it a moment before. Icicles hung from the ceiling like great stalactites, ready to impale you at a moment's notice.

At the head of the room, just before the dais, was the Winter queen, her hands outstretched and power dancing along her fingers. Before her, prone on the floor where before she had been so proud, was Dagmar. She had numerous cuts and contusions all over her body. At least one arm was broken. Her face was streaked with tears and her dark hair was nearly frozen over.

"You have *failed*," the queen snarled. She lashed out and scratched another gouge in Dagmar's shoulder. The human, the weak and pathetic human who had tried her very best to be strong in a court of beings who could eat her for breakfast, who could probably tear me in half with her bare hands, sobbed.

"I tried, my queen! We underestimated—"

"You *dare* criticise me!" Another slash, this time across Dagmar's back. "This was *your* failing!"

"I'm sorry," Dagmar pleaded. "I'll do anything! I can still—"

"You are a worthless human," the Winter queen

sneered. She lifted a foot and stomped on Dagmar's broken arm, making the woman scream loud enough to rattle the icicles. "What could you *possibly* do?"

"Enough!" I said. The Winter queen lifted her gaze to lock on me.

"You," she snarled. "I may not be able to *touch* you until you stand on Death's soil once more, but know this, Cal Thorpe: you are forevermore cursed to the Fae. The Seelie will hunt you and the Unseelie will feast on your bones. It will be our natures against yours, and you are nothing more than a worthless human. We will see you dead before dawn. This I swear. And twice again, I do swear. You will die."

I shrugged. "Wouldn't be the first time."

The Winter queen screamed at me, almost as bad as the banshee that I'd met in Chicago. She raised a finger at me in one of those ridiculously ominous postures that you see in bad horror movies. "Then you will watch *her* die."

In a flash of blinding snow, she and the whole castle holding the Fae of the Unseelie court vanished, leaving me in a familiar hilly field between the edges of a forest, the path to my freedom just behind me. And Dagmar, broken, bleeding, and abandoned, just before me.

13

LOYAL DOG

*D*agmar lay on the ground, her hand pressed to the wound in her side, staring up at me as if I either held all the answers, or was entirely to blame. Frankly, it could have been either.

Then, I saw something that made my very heart run cold, the strongest emotion I had felt since before my deal with Life, before the very thing that seemed to be both ripping me in half and holding me together. This was greater than my earlier wrath, greater than my dislike of being manipulated. I blinked furiously, hoping that the vision would vanish, that what I saw couldn't possibly be.

But it was.

A faint yellow-gold nimbus, starting to form around Dagmar's head, wrapping its fingers through her hair, brushing over her neck and embracing her bleeding, broken body like a lover. It was a sign of her imminent death, and I could see it because I truly was what I had hoped I wouldn't become. A Reaper.

I had been dithering about the whole thing, hoping I could stay just the way I was, and had become a Reaper anyways. I had told the wights what I was, and still believed that had been a bluff. I still felt the opposing powers of Life and Death working inside me, against each other, as close to a war as one could get. They, like the Fae, were stuck in that terrible cycle. Hating each other. Loving each other. Fighting each other. Neither ever able to get the upper hand. Just an eternity of conflict.

And I, foolish man that I was, had thought such conflict would save me.

Instead, I stood over Dagmar and watched her body bleed while that glowing nimbus formed and mist began to swirl around her body. There was no more denial left in me. I needed no emotion to tell me that.

I was a Reaper, and Dagmar was dying because of my actions and that stupid amulet in my pocket. I was *not* going to stand there and watch another friend die on me because of that amulet. Not like Charlotte. Not again.

Ignoring the blame in Dagmar's eyes, I crouched next to her and growled low in her face, my hair hanging over my eyes like a blanket, shielding me from her wrath. "I don't care what you think of me right now, Dagmar. I *can't* heal you or make you Fae. I don't know how. But you're not dead yet, and if you don't get off the ground and start moving, you're going to die. You said you knew plants that could kill you and plants that could save you. Well, Dagmar, the forest is just over there. Somewhere in that forest is a cure and I know it, and you know it. So you have a choice in front of you: either you lay here and I not only watch you die, I help it happen, or you roll over and *crawl* over to that forest and you make yourself a cure. Either you live, or you die. Your choice, Dagmar. Your very human, mortal, choice and the one thing you can never have if you become Fae. No one is making this one for you. No one is forcing you into a life you never wanted, nor one you wanted to escape."

Dagmar gritted her teeth together and ground something out, though it didn't sound like anything except desperate sounds to me. I couldn't touch her, not while the nimbus surrounded her. My Reaper abilities would just kill her. But I could get close.

The mist began to solidify into a thick, soupy sludge that obscured the forest from view. The temperature dropped and I knew, without a doubt, that the Winter queen had dropped us here on purpose. It was here, in the middle of these barrows, that I had proven to those watching Fae just how useful I actually was. This was where I had faced the monsters even the Fae feared and walked away. Now, I would watch those same monsters devour Dagmar while she bled out.

I heard whispers, moments away from being discernable words. They saw what I saw; the golden nimbus was pulsing, growing.

I bent my face closer to hers until we were literally inches apart. Her breath fogged up my glasses and I tore them off, Dagmar's proximity more than enough for me to see her clearly. Her eyes widened and her pupils, already dilated with impending death, fluctuated.

"Yeah, life sucks. Every day, there are an infinite number of choices laid out before you. It's impossible to run through them all, the consequences, the benefits. You'd go mad. I understand why you sold your life the way you did. It made things easier. But you can't run from Life, Dagmar. Can't run from Death, either. I've tried. It doesn't work, either way. You have to choose. Life, or Death. What do you want, huh? To know that you died pandering your existence to the whims of someone who cared nothing for you? Who abandoned you here to be devoured by wights? Or to *live*?"

Dagmar glared at me, taking in several deep breaths. The blood between her fingers didn't speed up in its progression, but neither did it slow. Her fingers, though, straightened and pressed harder over her wounds. She took one more gasping breath. "You bastard," she snarled.

"That's right," I snapped in return, hiding my relieved smile.

She whipped her head around so quickly I almost didn't have time to pull away. With a mighty heave, Dagmar turned herself over. With the arm not pressed to the wound on her side, she started dragging herself forwards, her toes scrabbling for purchase on the ground.

The whispers increased. I could understand them. The eagerness, the desperate hunger, that drove them to follow Dagmar and hunt her soul. I glared into the mist; it did not move any closer, but I doubted that my ire would hold them back for long. Our tentative detente would not last in the face of such temptation.

I stood and walked beside her. "You think that's the best you can do? Who taught you to fight like that?"

She gritted her teeth and pushed harder. The nimbus around her swelled, pulsing. I swallowed, mouth dry.

Then, the impossible. Dagmar reached the edge of the forest, suddenly visible through the mist. The wights screamed behind me, pushing closer until I could all but feel them pressing against my skin. They did not touch, for fear of what I would do to them, but when fear battled with hunger, hunger often won. Dagmar dragged herself another inch, grasping for a bunch of flowers, withered in the sudden drop of temperature.

I clenched my hands into fists, well beyond the point where I could possibly control my emotions. All thoughts of logic, of the passions surging within me likened to the weather as a passing fancy, gone. All that was left was primal, instinctual anger at those who had done this. Those who believed that they had the *right* to destroy someone like this just because they were powerful and she was not. They'd made me choose between all-out war and this destruction, and I'd made Dagmar choose what came next. Bastards indeed. It was the hardest thing she'd ever done and here I was, forcing her into it.

Dagmar gasped and stopped pulling herself forwards. She reached out with her free arm and pulled a plant from its roots, dragging it towards her. She tore off a leaf with her mouth and started chewing. Her golden nimbus grew larger. She reached for a flower, this time, chewing it as well, her eyes growing glazed. Then, Dagmar reached as far as she could, fingers stretching for that final plant, the one that would turn poison to cure. It was just out of reach.

I plucked the last plant from the ground and saw the hope in Dagmar's eyes die. I held it out to her, laying the leaves on the ground within an inch of her mouth. Desperately, her tongue darted out and lapped up the plant. She swallowed. Then, she stopped breathing.

I held my breath for as long as she did, staring at her as her eyes looked unseeing into the sky. The nimbus around her began to fade and I wondered if I had been too late. If, for once, the Reaper in me hadn't killed someone but simply waited for Death to come on his own.

"I'm sorry," I said. I repeated my apology, not sure if it was for Dagmar or for me.

Then, she started breathing again. "You bastard," she rasped, the words like treacle spilling from her mouth.

I laughed once. Twice. "Yeah. That's right."

"Thief, thrice over," the wights whispered behind me. "You would have us starve."

I glanced at Dagmar, at the glazed look in her eyes as the plants did what they were meant to do. Her wounds were still open, still bleeding, but it was slowing. I sank to the grass, that inane terror fading until my emotional state was nothing more than a still lake on a summer's day. Calm. Empty. The waters still frigid far beneath.

"I did not intend to intrude on your privacy," I told the wights. "I had not wanted to return."

"The dark queen sent you here," a slightly familiar voice said, still hissing with displeasure. "It is not a thing we can blame on you. Your thievery of a good meal, sending her beyond our borders...*that* we can blame on you."

I whistled out a deep breath. The wights pressed against me, their mist swirling around and yet never once touching my skin. My breath came into the air like steam from a bathhouse, and my fingers began to freeze, needles and pins taking over. Numbness would soon follow, I knew, and yet I remained where I was, watching Dagmar as she struggled with her own battle, an inch over the border.

Like a ripple across my thoughts, I wondered if I had done the right thing by forcing Dagmar to choose between Life and Death. Certainly, I had done no such thing. In fact, the two forces remained locked in chaotic battle within me, and my person, my being was locked in the middle.

I wondered, vaguely, how much of me would remain when their battle raged on and on. Would all that change when I found my soul, finally leaving me possessed of something to bolster my strength?

I pulled out the Eye of Carteria from my pocket and considered. "Do you know what this is?" I asked the wights. One wraith solidified to a point where I could almost see her figure clearly through the mist. She bent over and peered at the metal, moisture congealing on the metal.

"It is...old," was what she said.

"Older than the ground beneath your feet," another put in.

"Things like that do not survive such endless ages unless they contain the power to shake the world," the first agreed. None of this was news to me.

"I tried to lock it away, once, in the Library at Sazhem," I said.

"They would have been able to keep it, for a time," the second wight said, his voice deepening with a slight wobble. "But the Library is kept by the living, and they value power too much to lock it away forever."

"Then, in payment for my wrongs—intentional or otherwise—I entrust this to you, to guard as you guard the treasure of the ages." I turned my hand over the the amulet slipped from my fingers with an almost eerie ease. It thrummed with that tantalising power for a brief second as it hit the open air. I saw Dagmar's eyes widen and she nearly reached across the border to grab it, but her wounds were only barely starting to clot. It fell into the mist-born hand of the wights before she could do anything.

"It is done," the wights, those wraiths and wandering souls, said together. Then, in a swirl of mist, they were gone. We were left in a field of open grass and gentle hills, the air full of autumn bite but no more than that.

If I had thought a burden to be lifted from my shoulders by releasing the Eye, I was sorely mistaken. I felt no different than before.

Dagma groaned and rolled over, clutching her belly as the plants started to work. Incredibly, the wounds on her shoulder and side started to close, the blood soaking into the ground and disappearing. After a few minutes, the only sign that hse had been injured at all were the rends in her clothing. She sucked in great gasps of breath as the healing did its work, and it took me a moment to realise that she was crying.

Now that she wasn't in danger of dying at my touch, I sat next to her and wrapped my arm around her. "I'm sorry," I said once more. "I didn't know that my refusal to use the amulet was going to...I didn't know."

Dagmar shook her head desperately, her hair falling into her eyes. She pushed it aside with furious fingers. "I could have done it!" she insisted. "I could have done as she asked, had I only managed to take the amulet when I was supposed to. Now it is gone and I... I'll never be able to go back."

I took a deep breath and let it out slowly while Dagmar sniffled and sobbed. "I tried to use the amulet once, to save someone I cared about."

She eyed me and frowned. "Tried?"

I smiled faintly; of course she caught that turn of the phrase. She had been practically raised by Faeries, who were used to twisting their words. To manipulating. To violence. I nodded. "Yeah. Charlotte was caught as a champion to Life, and was fighting to survive against Death, too. I thought that if I captured her with the Eye, she wouldn't be bound to either. All I ended up doing was...let's just say that I wasn't strong enough."

Dagmar gaped at me and wiped her eyes with the back of her hand. "But you cannot die! You stood against my—against the Winter queen! You work for Death and Life. Surely you would be strong enough."

I shook my head. "No. And I don't think you would have been, either."

I saw that familiar stubbornness cross Dagmar's features and shook my head firmly.

"You could easily beat me into a pulp. I may not be able to die, but that does not mean I'm terribly handy in a fight. No, you are certainly strong, Dagmar, but this amulet was made and wielded by powers that could shape the world. I think, for all that you and I wish otherwise, we have to accept the fact that we're just...well, we're human."

Dagmar was silent for a few moments. The wind swirled around us, carrying the memory of winter's fury in its wake. I knew that I would have to start back home soon, if I wanted to meet Death when he returned. Not to mention, I had to place an order from an online pet supplier for ten of the best balls for Mayhem.

I climbed to my feet and brushed off my trousers. Dagmar scrambled up beside me, shaking her head furiously.

"I don't want to be Fae, anymore," she said. She cast a look in the direction of the depths of the forest and sniffed her last sniffle. She straightened her shoulders. "I thought she cared for me. I thought they all did."

"That's not in their nature." I shoved my hands into my pockets; it was getting colder. "And Fae are nothing if not bound to their nature."

"What am I bound to, now?" Dagmar asked. She stood there, appearing for all the world like a confident warrior ready to take on whatever monsters the world threw her way. She could probably fight Agravane under the table and she was certainly clever enough for Yolanda. I had a feeling, though, that offering her a job at my firm would be the easy way out. It didn't stop me from wanting to try.

"Look, Dagmar, I...There are a lot of wonders out there. A lot of things you could try and see, and I recommend that you do that. You've been working for the Fae for so long, falling in line with their expectations and machinations. You need to figure out just what it is that you want. I can't make you Fae. You'll have to—"

Dagmar waited a beat for me to pick up where I left off, then tilted her head in confusion. "What is it, Cal?"

"How did the Winter queen know that I could, theoretically, turn you Fae?" I asked. Dagmar frowned.

"She didn't," Dagmar said.

I shook my head, shoving my glasses up my nose and scowling fiercely. "No, she must have. Why else would she send me along on that ridiculous fetch and retrieve adventure with you, introducing the possibility of failure?"

"Because it was a pressing task that needed seeing to," Dagmar said. She sighed. "Even if that task was meant to start a war."

I held up a hand. "No, seriously, Shakespear and I added a huge element of instability into that plan. I work for *Death*. He's not bound to the Fae in any way, despite having two Faerie dogs and a Faerie cat as pets. Well, half-Faerie dogs. There was no guarantee that I would help your queen in her endeavours."

"You might not have figured it out," Dagmar said, wrapping her arms around herself. But she, too, was beginning to look unsettled.

"Yeah, but think about it. The Winter queen promised you life as a Fae if you completed this task, right? Right. And she couldn't actually turn you into a Fae—if she could, it would have been done a whole lot more, and made it into the legends, maybe."

Dagmar winced. "It's been done, but it usually

takes the death of another Faerie to achieve. It's unstable magic, changing someone's nature. She said that you were more stable. That you could do it without having to kill...she *must have* known, before you showed up. Before you came."

I nodded, my thoughts tingeing grim. "That's the thing, though. No one knew that I was coming to Faerie lands. I was only given the task of pet sitting the night before last. And Mischief and Mayhem running over the fence after the ball, then coming here? How could anyone predict that?"

"They are Faerie dogs," Dagmar said. She shrugged one shoulder in uncertainty. "Half-Faerie. But, still, the same boundaries on nature apply."

Which meant, near as I could figure, that someone who knew Mischief and Mayhem could easily manipulate them into running straight for Faerie territory, making me tag along. And who better at manipulation than a Faerie cat, a grimalkin, who was, by very nature, scheming and convinced of his superiority? He would have happily watched a war, secure in the knowledge that his side would win, because there was no way it couldn't.

I didn't realise that my hands were clenched into fists until they started trembling. I slowly relaxed my fingers, letting them uncurl. I refocused my attention and found Dagmar watching me, wary, one hand reaching towards the knife at her back. It was almost as if her near-death experience had never happened. She just ran from one crisis to the next, leaping from her position as the Winter queen's servant to helping me solve my problems because it was easier than trying to solve her own.

I forced a smile onto my face. "You have all of Elsewhere to explore. And the mortal realms, too, though I suggest you start small if you venture there. Avoid the cities. That sort of thing. You'll do well out there, Dagmar. I fully expect to be hearing about you on social media soon."

She frowned, confusion plying her features. "I don't understand. Are you not curious about—"

"No, Dagmar," I said. "That's my problem to deal with. You're free, now. Do what *you* want to do."

"But I want to help you!" she insisted. I refused again, shaking my head.

"No. Let me solve my problems. You look to yours. As nice as it is to have friends in this world, some things we need to do alone. But," and here I pulled out my phone—somehow, this device seemed to survive just about every situation I threw at it—"If you ever need something, or you just want to talk, give me a ring, alright?"

I held the device out to Dagmar, showing her my number. She looked at the screen and her mouth moved, twice, thrice, repeating the number over and over again until she had it memorised. When she handed my phone back, it was with trembling hands.

"I've never done anything on my own before," she admitted, as though the fact would astonish me or was in fact some shameful secret to be kept locked up.

"You'll figure it out," I promised. Then, without a goodbye or a backwards glance, because I knew that would only make it harder for her, I started to walk away, leaving Dagmar on the hill where the Fae had dumped her, determined to kill her.

Perhaps they had. The Dagmar they knew, the weak and subservient human, was no more. In her place was something entirely new. Unformed. Untamed. Unknown. But it was still Dagmar, nonetheless.

"Cal!" Dagmar called out. I paused. Debated turning. Sighed.

"Yes?" I asked, looking over my shoulder.

"You're going the wrong way," she said, pointing in a direction nearly opposite the one I had been about to take. I grinned and gave her a swift thumbs-up before turning and marching off in the new direction.

I needed to go have a conversation with Shakespeare about meddling in people's lives.

14

CAT'S PAW

Faerie must have been one of those stupidly annoying realms that shift each time a person walks through it. My journey to the border between Death's lands and the barrows took a mere ten minutes, though I fought plants and roots and puddles the whole way. I knew, objectively, that it should have taken hours, but it didn't. It was mildly unsettling to see the stream that marked the border only a short time after I had started my journey.

That did not stop me from crossing back into Death's lands and feeling relieved about it. The silvery-grey of the forest and its ivy settled over me like a familiar blanket. The air felt less charged, more still. I wasn't fighting with undergrowth or plants that would do their best to attack me. Instead, my path was smooth and sure.

My feet did hurt from where they had been banged

up by my ruined shoes letting twigs and rocks through, but that was merely an incidental physical sensation.

I ignored it.

The trek back to Death's house was, again, over before I felt it had really begun, and I was climbing over the fence into the sprawling back garden just as the sun began to touch the horizon, promising dusk. I wondered if Death had returned from his jury duty. I think it would have been better if he had; we could have a nice, civilised conversation with Shakespeare about the nature of meddling, sipping brandy—and coffee—next to the fire.

If he hadn't returned, my authority was limited and I rather imagined that we would have a far less polite conversation.

I made it all the way to the back door before being found out, and then it was simply Mischief and Mayhem coming to barrel me over. I was on my back before you could say "trice", dog tongues doing their best to take my face off.

"You have returned," Mischief said, her whole body wagging with indefatigable pleasure. She wined and rolled to the ground, letting me scratch her belly. Of course, as soon as I did that, Mayhem had to get in on the fun, his slightly bigger build shoving Mischief out of the way until they were wrestling each other, trying to decide who got first dibs on my attention.

"Relax, you two," I said, holding up my hands. "I have two hands. I can pet you both."

Immediately, the dogs pressed against my side, tails

still wagging ferociously. "We are glad you are not dead, Cal. Or, well, seriously injured, since you cannot die."

That confirmed my suspicions about Shakespeare knowing my particular skillset. I scratched the dogs behind the ears and Mischief let out a whine of pure ecstacy. "Death tells you about me, huh?"

"Oh, yes," Mayhem said, his jaw dropping open and his tongue lolling. "Death thinks you are a very interesting person. And he said that you would be very good about playing with us and feeding us, because he left you instructions and we were good dogs."

"You *are* good dogs," I agreed. "I'm sorry you got into all this trouble."

Here, they stopped wagging their tails. Mischief put her ears back and exchanged a glance with Mayhem. He whined, lowering his tail. "We were bad," he said. "We should not have jumped the fence."

"You are half-Faerie, are you not?" I asked. Mischief nodded, pressing her shoulder closer to my thigh. "And you are dogs, too. Being both means that you are bound by your nature as Fae—to return to Faerie and be amongst your people, as required of your court loyalties. And also bound to your nature as dogs to chase after the ball, right?"

Both dogs nodded, though they still looked upset. I crouched down and looked them both in the eyes, receiving another bath of dog germs to the face. "Right. So, while you shouldn't have jumped the fence, you were only doing what your nature says to do. Next time, though, try to be more loyal dog and less Fae."

"Okay," Mischief said, giving me one more lick. Mayhem nodded vigorously.

"We play now?" he asked, tail wagging once more. I shook my head, though I scratched behind their ears for a few more moments.

"No. Now I need to go have a conversation with Shakespeare," I said. The dogs whined, both of them putting their ears back.

"Shakespeare is dangerous," Mischief said, her voice barely a whisper. "He does not play nice games. He likes being in charge and making things work the way he wants them to work. It is bad."

"Does Death know?" I asked, more out of mild curiosity than anything.

"Yes." Mayhem nodded.

"No." Mischief shook her head.

The two dogs exchanged a glance and let out a sigh as one. "It's complicated," I translated. My guess was that Death knew of Shakespeare's nature and tolerated it, as he tolerated my own difficulties, and Yolanda's, and Agravane's. All were equal to Death. It was not his role to change their life, only to be present in it.

I patted the dogs once more on the head before moving towards the back of the house. The door was wide open from the morning before; a smattering of leaves sat over the threshold, though the rest of the kitchen was spotless. I waited until the dogs were in before closing the door and locking it firmly behind them. Then, I looked about for Shakespeare.

In true cat fashion, he was nowhere in sight, only likely to be found when he wanted to be found. Luckily for me, I knew that in spite of all his arch comments and snide remarks, the power he thought he wielded and the machinations that he had set into motion, there was one thing he just couldn't do: open the treat bag.

I wandered to the counter, where the animals' food and treats had been set out. I took enough time to fill Mischief and Mayhem's food bowls. The dogs set to, scarfing down the food as though they were starving. Then, sure to rustle the plastic, I opened the bag of cat treats with a snap.

A few moments later, Shakespeare sauntered in. He yawned, as though he had just woken from a nap, stretching and showing off his claws. Mayhem growled lightly as the cat got too close to his food. Shakespeare ignored him.

The grimalkin leaped to the countertop, wrapping his tail neatly around his paws as he stared at the bag of treats. "You made it home, then," he mewed.

I considered the bag of treats in my hand, even going so far as to read the ingredients on the back. Shakespeare narrowed his eyes. "You know," I said, carefully resealing the bag and setting it on the counter, "I don't really think you deserve these."

Shakespeare hissed, showing all his fangs in a very

obvious threat. "Did I not fulfil my bargain?" he snarled.

I shrugged and scratched my side. "You did. Granted, you neglected to inform me of the fact that we were in Faerie to begin with because you wanted me there. You had, what, made a promise to deliver me to the Winter queen, supposedly secure in the knowledge that I could turn humans to Fae? You thought I would cooperate with her scheme to start a war? Well, Shakespeare, for all your planning and your cleverness, you truly know nothing about humans."

Shakespeare rose from sitting and bared his fangs at me, his tail arching high above his head, his hackles raised. From their positions on the floor, the dogs started growling. I waved them off.

"You are not human," the grimalkin said flatly. "You should have done exactly what I intended."

"Well, I hate to break it to you, but I'm still human. Maybe something else, too, but I still have that mortal unpredictability and potential that you Faeries so crave and yet can't have." I leaned close to the spitting cat and, for once, he was the one to back a step up. Alarm flashed in his eyes. "And I really, really hate being manipulated."

In an instant, the Faerie cat lunged for me, claws extended. Only a blood-deep instinct had me raising my arm and taking the brunt of the blow on my forearm. I reached for Shakespeare, intending to grab his neck or his ruff or anything I could use to pin him down. Instead, he latched his teeth deep into my wrist, sending jolts of bright agony up my arm.

I screamed.

Shakespeare yowled as I shook my arm violently and threw him across the kitchen. He hit the wall and fell to the ground, landing perfectly balanced and spitting fury. "You *worthless* human! Do you know what you have done?!"

"I stopped you from tearing this world to pieces," I said, cradling my wounded arm. Mischief and Mayhem stepped in front of me, teeth showing, keeping Shakespeare from attacking me again. He hissed and lashed his tail.

"You know nothing of it! It would have been glorious, to see the battle, to taste blood as has not been spilled in a generation. You don't know how this world —and *your* world—was shaped, over and over again, by people who held the power of the stars in their claws! I *handed* you that power, and you wanted to lock it away!" Shakespeare was screaming, now, his voice echoing off the rafters and setting the pots of the kitchen to rattling.

"What gives you the right to try and reshape the world?" I demanded. My arm and wrist throbbed and I was fairly certain that I was bleeding onto the floor, but I didn't dare look away from Shakespeare, from the challenge that he sent my direction.

"I was *born* with that right," he snapped. He took a step forwards, growling low in his throat at the dogs as they stood in his way. Mischief faltered for a moment, stepping backwards with her claws scrabbling on the tile. Mayhem returned Shakespeare's growl with one of his own, deep enough to shake the floor.

Shakespeare swiped a claw at Mayhem, but didn't strike. "I am a symbol of Death. I am born in the squall of blood and I have the magic of witches running through my veins, ready to be used. And what do I do with my life? While it away, lounging in front of a fire, waiting for my *master* to return and deign to pet me, to feed me, to give me treats. I once stood at the side of *conquerers* and warmongers, people who would shape the world in their image. And yet you think that I was named after that ridiculous playwright and his slippery tongue. No, I was here long before him, but *he* is the one known. Not I. Not Death's little pet."

I shifted my weight and noted, idly, that I was becoming lightheaded. If I didn't see to the massive gashes on my arm, soon, then I would likely faint and Shakespeare would be free to go off and do, well, supervillain activities. "Your arrogance does not suit you, Shakespeare," I said, voice acidic in my mouth. "The age of the world shaping is *over*. We humans don't need you to guide us anymore. And your war? The one you wanted to break the balance and remake the world? It's never going to happen. The Eye is gone."

Shakespeare's eyes grew and his ears flattened. His tail whipped from side to side and he dug his claws into the tile with a ferocious screech. "What have you done?" he breathed.

"Oh, you thought that I would just return with the

amulet? That I would leave it lying around for anyone to find? Or, perhaps you thought that you could convince me to use it, to test it out again and see if I could master it after failing the first time." I snorted and instantly realised that was a bad idea. My light-headedness was turning into full-on vertigo and if I hadn't been bracing my weight against the counter, I was fairly certain that I would have fallen over. "I left it where no one will find it. Not you, not your precious Unseelie, not even other humans."

Shakespeare let out a yowl that forced Mischief and Mayhem back, pawing at their ears to defend against the rage of a creature like the grimalkin. I realised, now, that ever thinking of him as a cat was a mistake. He was rage and arrogance incarnate. He was the furious companion of gods like the Morrigan, yet he fought against even that binding. He was someone who knew himself superior and was still bound to others. To his nature as a Faerie. He was eager for blood and for death. He wanted to remake the world and finally take the power that he thought to be his right. His nature demanded such action.

And this stupid, ignorant, useless human dared to stand in his way.

Shakespeare gathered his haunches beneath him and made a marvellous leap towards me, his claws outstretched and reaching for my throat. He flew at me with murder in his eyes and I knew, then, that he was going to kill me. Then, when I came back, he was going to kill me again. And again. And again. Until such time as he had sated his thirst for blood on my never-ending supply.

Frankly, I thought that was a terrible idea.

I ducked.

I read somewhere that house cats were some of the most effective hunters in the cat world; they managed to take down more prey than their larger relatives and were, generally, a huge difficulty to the songbird population. Now, I was most certainly not a songbird, but neither was Shakespeare your average house cat.

Thirty-some-odd pounds of furious cat launched at me and managed to turn almost gracefully as I ducked. I felt his claws pass overhead, splitting the air and nearly catching me in their terrible clutches. Before I could recover and do something intelligent, like run away, Shakespeare was already clawing his way up my back. The points dug into my skin through my sweater and the grimalkin clawed gouges into my flesh.

They weren't nearly as deep as the cuts on my forearm, or the punctures from his fangs on my wrist, but it hurt just as badly. I did not have to feel emotion to know that.

I screeched and turned desperately, trying to reach around and grab Shakespeare to haul him off of my shoulders. All I managed to do was stretch the gouges and split more skin. Shakespeare chuckled darkly in my ear.

"Finally, I will do what I am made for," he purred, reaching out to drag his claws across my face.

"Get off of Cal!" Mayhem snarled, finally entering

the fray. Mischief let out a bark of distress and raced from the kitchen, her paws carrying her swiftly towards safety. I did not blame her one bit for doing that. The dogs were very capable, sure, but this was Shakespeare they were fighting. And that grimalkin ruled the house with an iron paw.

Mayhem did something I couldn't see, his movements jostling me so that the cuts on my back burned harder. A moment later they soothed and I realised that Mayhem must have torn Shakespeare from my back. I rose to my full height and turned to face the fray, full of vicious barking and the yowling of felines.

Mayhem was held down by his nose, Shakespeare's claws perilously close to his eyes. The Faerie cat raised a paw to strik Mayhem down, his tail lashing and his teeth bared in a remorseless gaze.

I lunged forwards, using perhaps one of the few useful self-defence moves that Agravane had taught me, balancing my weight and throwing it intentionally at a target. My good hand met Shakespeare's side with a *thud* and he staggered backwards, shaking his head to clear the sudden change in orientation.

I stood over Mayhem, who whined and growled. "Don't you dare," I said, voice low.

"Who are you to stop me?" Shakespeare spat. "Some insignificant human, who was made what you are by a mistake! You hold no more sway over the universe than that fool human Dagmar. The Winter queen should never have trusted her to do her bidding.

She should have entrusted the task to someone capable, someone who would not fail her!"

I snorted. "I hate to break it to you, but you wouldn't have been able to complete the task any more than Dagmar. Guess what, Shakespeare? For all you live with Death, you are still bound by your nature."

Shakespeare hissed, crouching down. "My nature is to kill," he said and launched himself at me again.

I raised my good hand to defend myself and staggered back two steps when Shakespeare's bulk slammed into me. He writhed in my grip and the force overwhelmed my balance. I fell backwards, slamming my injured back into the tile floor. My head swam as it bounced on the tile. Humans were really not well equipped for fighting Faeries, I decided.

Shakespeare raised his head triumphantly, eyes flashing. He opened his jaws and I knew that he was going to tear out my throat and there would be nothing I could do to stop him. Mayhem yelped in the corner, but even the dog could not get to me fast enough.

Shakespeare lowered his head, the moment seeming to float between two heartbeats. Then, suddenly, liquid—water, with just a hint of vinegar—spritzed over the two of us and broke us both out of the reverie of the battle. I winced at the touch of vinegar in my wounds and Shakespeare screeched in horror, flinging himself backwards and huddling against the base of the counter, ears pressed flat against his head, hissing.

More liquid sprayed at Shakespeare and the cat

shook his head vigorously to try and dispel the offending liquid. I blinked several times to try and clear my vision and saw Death, looking dapper as usual with his pinstripe three-piece suit and bright crimson cravat, his expression thunderous. He was holding a bright blue spray bottle, about half-full of that water-vinegar mixture, and sprayed Shakespeare twice more.

"*Bad* cat!" Death said, something close to true anger in his voice.

Shakespeare hissed once more and received a mouthful of water and vinegar for his efforts. Spitting, ears pinned back and tail low, he slunk from the kitchen without a backward glance, his very posture the epitome of consternation.

When he was gone, Mayhem stepped over me and started licking my face. Mischief stood near him, her tail wagging and her tongue lolling. "Master is home," she said proudly.

"I see that pet sitting was rather more dramatic than I intended," Death said, reaching out and holding up a hand. I took it, wincing as the physical pain over-rode any emotional turmoil, no matter how strong.

"That spray bottle wasn't in the instructions," I said, my voice little more than a rasp. Death took one good look at me, at the torn sweater and my ruined arm, the blood dripping down my back, and frowned. He pulled out a phone—the first one I'd ever actually seen him use—and pressed a few buttons, holding it to his ear.

"Hello, Yolanda. Yes, I have returned from jury duty. No, I...well, as it turns out, it's rather pointless to sit on a murder trial when I know who the real killer was. Yes. Actually, if you wouldn't mind fetching Doctor Graveltoes here, I believe Cal requires some patching. Yes, again. Very well." Death rang off and slipped the phone back into the inner pocket of his jacket.

I waited for him to say something, swaying slightly as my heart pounded and pushed further blood out of my wounds. Vaguely, I realised that he *was* actually talking and that I had simply not registered any of it.

"I think you had better wait until the Doc has seen me," I said, a hint of my firm logical nature showing through, appearing now that my emotions were dulled. I frowned at that, thinking that the oddly logical personality hadn't appeared since Life had "stabilised" me. In fact, the two warring forces within me were quieting, pushed back by the physical pain, and by something else entirely.

I blinked and rubbed my eye, pulling my hand back a moment later when I realised that it was, in fact, still wet from the water and vinegar mixture. Like a dragon or some other terrible beast, the forces within me growled at the discomfort of vinegar to the eye, then settled.

"I think there might be something else wrong," I admitted to Death. His brows winged up in surprise, then I very firmly blacked out.

15

DOG TIRED

I woke to a very familiar sight, given my experiences in Elsewhere. I was laying in bed—mine, I think—feeling like the world had chewed me up and spit me out, with large, bulbous eyes staring down at me from an all too close vantage point. I gurgled in surprise and the small creature clambered off my chest to jump to the floor.

Doc Graveltoes was one of the few physicians in Elsewhere. Oh, there were healers a plenty, but Graveltoes was a true physician, though how he attended medical school, I have no idea. He worked on all the species of Elsewhere, but as many of them were magically enhanced or outright immortal, his services were often under utilised.

Or, they had been until I came along. I seemed to find myself under his care quite frequently. Hence the intense staring.

"You are better," Graveltoes said definitively,

moving about my room while he cleaned up bandages and other medical detritus. I grumbled and sat up, leaning against my headboard. A quick mental check confirmed Graveltoes' diagnosis; I was, in fact, much better.

I held up my arm and turned it over, looking for signs that I had been wounded by a grimalkin earlier that day. At least, I assumed it was the same day. But as I examined my arm, the scars I found there were months old lines of silver that did not even twinge when I poked at them. My back was similarly unaffected by pain.

I looked dubiously at Graveltoes. The goblin-gremlin creature sighed and leaped up to my bed again, coming at me with one of those things you use to examine eyes. He pulled my glasses from my nose and shone a light at me, making me wince. With a grunt and a nod, Graveltoes returned my glasses. I perched them on my nose.

"So...fully healed," I said. "That's pretty cool, right?"

"Pah! Cat scratches. Graveltoes is the most renowned doctor in Elsewhere, and they have him healing cat scratches! It is an insult." He tossed some of the bandages and things into a small bag and stomped around the room, cleaning up the rest.

"Thank you," I said. Graveltoes just grunted and hunched his shoulders then left, muttering and stomping the whole way.

Death passed the irate doctor as he came in,

wearing the same suit and cravat and confirming my suspicions that very little time had passed. Death shook his head good naturedly and closed the door behind him. "He seems to be in a mood."

"I think he was disappointed at my lack of serious injury," I said, holding up my now-healed arm for Death to see. "Apparently being attacked by a grimalkin is boring."

Death chuckled. "I doubt that you think so."

I thought about joining in the light banter, thinking that it might lighten the mood, but something inside me kept silent. I waited for Death to approach. He waved a hand and a comfortable club chair, the twin to the ones he kept in his study, materialised at my bedside. Death sank into it with a quiet exhale, folding his hands before him.

"Before you ask," I said, "maybe you should explain why the energies—yours, and Life's—aren't there anymore. I mean, I can feel *something*, but it isn't what it was before."

"And what was it before?" Death asked, a strange interest in his voice. He brushed his knee, straightening the line of his trousers. It was a casual move, and yet strangely calculated.

I lowered my gaze to the duvet, a pleasant charcoal colour that I had always found soothing. Now, it was just another shadow on my thoughts. I considered as I ran my hand over the fabric. "Before, it was like being in a room with the two of you when you're having a tiff. Like two irresistible forces pulling at me from either side. I literally could not move one way or another. I think that's why I could feel things more like normal, rather than being tied by logic or passion. Things were still unstable, but they were...steady. If that makes sense."

Death nodded, the motion smooth and elegant, a dark power acknowledging a truth. "It does. That describes, almost exactly, what my relationship with my wife is like. Unstable, but steady. Those were our powers fighting within you. Your contract with me, and your agreement with Life, pulling at you for attention. Very well, what is it like, now?"

I licked my dry lips, squinting as I tried to come up with the words to explain precisely what it was I felt. "It's like...shadow. And mist. And hunting in the dark. Exhilarating. Terrifying. But it is one thing, like a being inside me, a part of me that is...more. And yet, dependent on me being as I am."

Death nodded again, though this time I could tell that his attention was not on me, but was considering my words. He tilted his head and said nothing for a moment, the empty spaces that were his eyes focused on something far in the distance. Then, with whip-like intensity, he snapped his attention back to me. "I think you had better tell me what happened while I was gone."

I scowled, running back over the situation of the last couple of days. I started at the beginning and didn't stop once, though my voice nearly gave out from talking. When I was done, feeling the memory of pain in my arm, Death handed me a glass of water that he'd definitely not had a few moments before. I drank it down swiftly, the coolness soothing my thoughts as much as my energy.

I set the glass on the nightstand and waited.

Death took a deep breath, the intake of air moving his shoulders upwards. When he exhaled, the tension remained. "The Fae—at least, those of the Celtic variety, as you met—have a dark and bloody background. Their bloodlust used to be tempered on mortals, like your friend Dagmar, but when Elsewhere was firmly separated from the mortal realm, even after the creation by means of the Eye, their access to their prey became limited. You surmised that those who dwelt in the mortal realms were the weaker of their kind, living amongst humans. You are partly wrong."

I thought of Dermot Green, the fetch I had assisted only a short while ago. he hadn't seemed stronger than the Fae I encountered; if anything, he was remarkably human-like.

"The Fae that you met are bound by their natures in a way that is almost enslavement. They cannot go against what they are. Those in the mortal realms have more freedom to bend their natures, to adapt, to take on some of the free will and potential that the mortals possess. It is a heady power, and the Fae here taste it but rarely. Thus, they become little more than mindless extensions of what they were made. Intelligent, yes. Manipulative, yes. But mindless all the same.

"Life and I are also nature-bound, but we are far

more powerful than the Fae. We create our natures. They were created for their natures. And Shakespeare was and is a creature of bloodshed and death. The Fae thought to bind Shakespeare to me because I *am* Death, but they failed to take into account that I am more than they can understand or pin down. Because of it, Shakespeare languishes here."

Death held out his hands in a resigned shrug. He lifted his chin and studied the painting I had above my bed; it was a piece of greyscale photography, a gaslight lampost dissolving into the mist on a cobbled street. It was a picture of home, meant to remind me of where I came from. Death smiled sadly at it and lowered his gaze.

"I am sorry for what happened. I...In my own arrogance, I assumed that some time with someone different, away from me and the fact that I am more than he, would help Shakespeare. Perhaps grant him a different perspective. For all my desire, my abilities with the living, even those attuned to me, are...poor."

I barked out one terse laugh. "I think he just saw an opportunity to prove his superiority."

Death smiled wanly. "It was a mistake, and one that I shall not be making again. I think it time that Shakespeare return to his home. It will be a difficult transition, but better for him. For me."

Part of me felt badly, like this separation between pet and master was somehow my fault. I hated to see a family like that broken up. The rest of me, though, the part that remained rational knew that Shakespeare was not a tame cat, not a being that could be forced into that role. He was too wild, and he would either suffer for it, or die. Returning him to the Fae to fight his own battles was the best option.

But, in all of this explanation, I still didn't understand what had happened to me. I eyed Death, wondering if he would tell me of his own volition or if I would have to drag the answer out of him about this strange new presence that lived within me. Or, the thing that set my thoughts to stillness, what if he didn't know?

"I can feel you thinking," Death said, crossing his ankle over his knee. He appraised me again for a moment. "I have an answer for you, Cal, but I do not know if you will like it."

"Just tell me." Emotion, weak though it was, broke over me and seemed to solidify the more I considered the presence, the thing, inside me. It turned over and regarded me with a careful eye. I returned the favour.

"Your Reaper abilities have come into fruition."

I nodded, waiting. Death said nothing more, just watched me as if I would do something really annoying like start tearing out my hair or gnashing my teeth. Instead, I just shrugged. "Well, yeah. I knew that. I figured it out when I was watching Dagmar die."

Death held up a long finger, shadows swirling around it. One of them broke off and moved about me as if curious. It lingered for a moment on my new scars before returning to Death. He blinked and settled his hand back in his lap. "But you did not simply *watch*

Dagmar die. You presented her with a choice. The thing is, Cal, that while I am the one who utilises Reapers the most, they are just as much a creature of Life as of me. They are beings who exist in the liminal spaces between moments. They stand between Life, and Death. They do not interfere as such, shaping the world to their whims, but present a path. A crossroads. Humans associate Reapers with me because dying is one of the largest crossroads a person can face. But sometimes, fear of a Reaper is enough to entice them to choose a new path. It is not the only place where Reapers can be present, though. Any choice can call you, if the need is significant enough."

I frowned at this. It all sounded rather more ridiculous than Death had first led me to believe. A space between moments? A crossroads? What was this, some high-brow television series? Since stating that thought would be incredibly rude, and since I wasn't entirely sure that this thing inside me—this thing that might well have *been* me—wasn't what Death claimed, I asked a different question. "So making that deal with Life, was like some sort of preordained step in becoming a Reaper?"

Death chuckled at this. I was glad to see that someone was amused at this. I certainly wasn't.

"Your running to Life was not preordained. You are still human, Cal, if also possessed of power that is not often seen in one of mortal blood. As a human, your ability to choose your fate is perhaps the most coveted power of all. And you chose to go to Life. Granted, this act may have accelerated the process of your power coming into being, manifesting, but it wasn't the cause."

I could feel the start of a headache coming on. I pressed my fingers to my temples and massaged my head, trying to sort out the myriad of thoughts. I settled on one, the one that had stuck with me since discovering this whole Reaper situation to begin with. "What about my soul?"

Death shrugged, casual. "What about your soul?"

"Does being a Reaper mean that I'll never get it back? Am I going to feel this weak version of emotion forever? I can't even tell if this state of being is real, or if I'm imagining what I'm feeling. Am I happy? Sad? Weary? I want to say yes to all of them, but I don't know why!"

Here, Death stood and tugged at the edges of his suit, putting it back into its proper lines. The club chair vanished as if it had never been and I knew, without a single shred of doubt, that I wasn't going to get the answers that I wanted.

"You are still human," Death said again. "Humans have souls."

I had to ask, though, as more questions rose to the forefront of my mind. I managed one, barely louder than the others. "So this...thing inside me, it's just a mixture of your power and Life's? It's not...alive, like it feels?"

Death chuckled, the sound dark and with just a hint of pleasure. "Life and I may be married, Cal, but our powers do not combine without some very significant consequences. If they have indeed melded into your Reaper abilities, rather than merely triggering them, I would not expect things to be quite so simple as you hope."

With that super helpful piece of advice, Death turned and strode to the door. He paused, but did not look back over his shoulder. "Get some rest, Cal. Your journey has barely begun."

Death closed the door behind him and I groaned, falling back into my pillow with a *whump*. Sometimes—not often, but sometimes—I really hated my boss.

Then, there was a knock on my door and the Morrigan swanned in, and I really wished my boss would come back and tell her off. I settled into my pillow and folded my arms, the creature lurking just beneath my skin writhing with displeasure.

"We meet again," the Morrigan said.

"By no choice of my own. You know, you're supposed to wait for permission before entering after you knock," I said, sniffing in disdain. The Morrigan laughed and sat perched at the end of my bed by my feet. She ran her hands over the duvet.

"Wasn't I done with you? Didn't you tell me to mind my own business back in Faerie? Or do you want to chastise me for preventing a war, oh battle goddess?" I'm fairly certain that the level of sarcasm in my voice could have scalded bare skin. The Celtic goddess just regarded me with a wicked smile.

"The Fae were but one challenge that faced you

this day," she said with all the pompous arrogance of one who holds power and knows precisely how to wield it. "Their war would have been devastating."

I was tempted to glower, but that would reveal just how much I disliked this situation. I considered, then gave in, glowering as fiercely as I could manage, the *thing* within me doing the same, a hiss of power flooding my veins. "You stopped the Summer Queen so they wouldn't go to war as they were. I noticed that you weren't there when the Winter queen wanted to start a war with the sides unbalanced."

The Morrigan smiled, and made me absolutely certain that she wasn't human. She had the look of someone who had seen the bloodshed of the ages and did not care that more was to come. She tilted her head and I could have sworn that I saw a hint of feathers just beneath her skin, her eyes black and eager.

"I gave you the tools that you required to solve the problem on your own."

I really hated it when people said things like that. It was well deserving of the eye-roll that I gave her. "Oh, yes, that's supremely helpful," I grumped. "Seriously, though, why did you interfere the first time and not the second? Frankly, the thought of an unbalanced war is more terrifying than a balanced one. If anything, I would have thought that you—"

"Do not presume to know me, or even the Fae. You have had dealings with them, yes, but their natures extend back centuries. They are not so easily pinned as you might thing," the Morrigan said, her expression hardening. I very nearly rolled my eyes again.

"I'm fully aware that pretty much everything in Elsewhere is older than me, thanks." I reached behind me and fluffed my pillow, settling in with all the arrogance of an invalid, even if I was perfectly healthy after my healing. "What I want to know is why."

"Why what?" She flashed me a wicked grin.

"If you weren't going to interfere the second time, then why interfere at all? It stinks of falling into archetypes and patterns, and I don't like it," I said. The Morrigan opened her mouth to speak, but I kept going. I was getting rather good at this talking and reasoning thing, and I wasn't going to stop, now. "You aren't Fae. From all that I've heard, the Fae are maybe descended from your people, or your enemies, or *their* enemies. But you are certainly not Fae. Okay, sure, you might have felt obligated to interfere because you both share an origin, but that doesn't make sense, either. You interfered on *my* behalf, for all your talk of stopping a war. I want to know why."

There was a pause, pregnant as I'll get out, and we regarded each other for a moment. The Morrigan watched me, her dark eyes shifting every so often as if she were examining me in different light spectrums. The being inside of me, whatever it really was, uncurled enough to open a great eye, bright and glowing and yellow. Precisely the colour of the nimbus I saw surrounding the dying.

It seemed like the two beings locked gazes and then

recoiled from each other, snarling. The Morrigan recovered first, smoothing her battle dress with a casual touch. My beast thing took a few more moments to settle, writing uncomfortably inside me until I was fairly certain I was going to lose my lunch, despite not having had any.

I closed my eyes and forced the feeling down. The thing quieted, acquiescing, for now, to my authority.

"How very interesting," the Morrigan purred. She inhaled, as if taking my scent, which was quite creepy. "I wondered what would happen when your power awoken, young Reaper, and I am not disappointed."

Then, just like Death, she rose, dusted herself off, and strode from my room without a backwards glance. I couldn't even form a question before she was gone, once again. I had the sickening feeling that this whole thing, from start to finish, had been nothing but pure manipulation to get me to become whatever it was that I had become. Why?

Because the older beings of Elsewhere, these Elderkin like the Morrigan, were curious.

Well, in the world of marketing, the only way to quell curiosity is to give them all a story they could digest. It didn't have to be the truth, though that was usually better, but it had to be believable.

I lay back on my pillow and pulled out my phone, plugging it in to the charger on my nightstand. Then, I began crafting my story.

16

CATURDAY

"Hey, Cal."

I looked up from where I had been resting my head against my front door. I'd forgotten that Neja was meant to meet up with me today. She looked good, her petite figure decked out in a black jumpsuit, a black leather jacket slung over her shoulders. Her silvery hair was tied back in a tail and her grey-blue skin was practically glowing with power. She looked dangerous and capable. As a private investigator and bounty hunter to the magical world, she was both of those things, and clever besides.

I liked Neja. She also scared me a bit.

"Hey, Neja," I said in greeting. "I'd let you in, but I left my key inside this morning and some poltergeists locked me out. Actually, I think they just changed the locks entirely, but...anyways, the locksmith won't be here for another two hours."

Neja nodded, looking at the door. "Are you particularly attacked to your door? Does it have any emotional significance?"

"I mean, it's a nice door," I said, looking at the solid maple door, stained a pleasant tea color. "But, no, there's no—"

Neja lifted her leg and struck out. I jumped out of the way at the last possible moment, caught completely unawares. Thank goodness my instincts were turned to flight in the whole fight-or-flight scenario, or I would have had a nasty bruise in a rather unfortunate area. Neja's kick was seriously precise and obviously had some power behind it. She hit the door just below the locking mechanism, and it cracked open like an explosion.

Neja strode through the now-open door as though she'd done nothing at all. I gaped at the ruined splinter of my doorframe, perhaps more astonished that the door itself seemed perfectly intact.

"Can you teach me to do that?" I asked, following her. Neja shrugged off her jacked, revealing bare arms, and threw the piece of clothing across the back of my couch. She collapsed into the cushions like she deserved to be there, and rested her head on the back of the couch with a groan.

"Ask me again after Agravane's had a chance to train you," she said. "Do you have anything to drink? I have had a really strange last few days."

"Um, I've got—"

"*Not* coffee." She lifted her head long enough to glare at me with silver eyes.

"I was going to say whisky," I replied with a sniff.

Neja sat up straight on the couch, every muscle tense, eyes wide and jaw dropped. "Wow," she said. I waited, half-expecting what was going to come next. She narrowed her eyes at me. "You look different. You're acting different. What happened?"

I fiddled with the whiskey and the cut-crystal tumblers, hunching my shoulders. I poured us both a generous portion and sat on the couch, handing her one of the glasses. Neja took a hefty sip, but did not take her eyes from me for a moment. "Have...have you heard of Reapers?" I asked.

"Well, yeah. They're old legends, said to have died out centuries ago. Even by Elsewhere standards, these guys were something to comment on. Supposedly existed in the in between places, the places that not many beings had the power to go. Mostly associated with Death, but could appear at any major crossroads." Neja took another drink, considering. She nodded and tapped her chin with her glass. "I don't know a whole lot; they're mostly just stories at this point. What I have heard, though, tells me they're sort of a last resort for most people. Why do you ask? Did you meet one?"

I stared into the amber liquid in my glass. Even with my emotions still muted, this seemed like a bad idea. Maybe I shouldn't say anything. "You said you had a strange couple of days?" I asked instead.

"Cal," Neja said.

I smiled weakly, but didn't look at her.

"Cal," Neja said again, this time with more force

behind the word. I lifted my gaze and met hers square on. When I did, just like it had with the Morrigan, the thing inside me churned and lifted its head. It opened an eye, then closed it and opened the other, looking firmly at Neja. She stared back at me, and cursed. Loudly.

"Stars above, Cal!" Neja practically flew to a standing position, the whisky tumbler suddenly resting on the coffee table when it hadn't been there before. "What *happened*?"

I lay my head back and stared up at the ceiling. "Frankly? I have no idea. I was acting as Death's proxy, and something woke up. Death said I was becoming a Reaper, so I ran to Life to try and stabilise my condition. That, apparently, set off a *different* chain reaction, which led to not only me becoming a Reaper, but creating this...this...thing. I've been calling it Sebastian."

Neja snorted. "Only you, Cal, would call the living entity that is your power '*Sebastian*'. I mean, do you even know what it is?"

I shook my head. Neja sat back down on the couch and drained the rest of her whisky. I handed her my tumbler, and she drained that, too. "Apparently, I'm not a normal Reaper, if even there was such a thing. Death says that things aren't ever simple when his power and Life's actually get together."

"I think that might be an understatement," Neja agreed. She looked at Sebastian again, her power roving over mine, then shifted her gaze so that she just looked at me, no power, just me. "You know, I used to think that I got into strange situations. That my job was unusual and that I often saw the weirdest that Elsewhere had to offer. I think you might win that title, though."

I sighed. "Goodie."

"So what about your soul?" Neja asked. I knew what she was asking, because I had asked Death the same thing. I told her what he'd said. She snorted again. "Seriously?! You're *still* human?!"

I shrugged. "I mean, it's not like there's a manual for these things. I still feel off, like the part of me that feels things, that should be able to do normal, human things, is missing. I think it's because the soul is unique to humans, just like our potential to choose and without my soul, that part of me is sort of...dormant, or really hard to access."

Neja's brows winged up. "Well, you certainly *have* thought about this."

"I've spent a couple of days dealing with the Fae. They really clarify the whole mortal potential thing."

"Well, I hate to break it to you, but you mortals aren't the only ones with that potential. You are certainly the strongest of the chaos beings, but not the only ones. Still, that's a discussion for another time." Neja reached behind her and grabbed her jacket, fiddling with the pockets. She pulled out a piece of plastic, maybe four inches by two inches, with a piece of nearly-disintegrated paper sandwiched between its layers.

She fanned herself with the piece for a moment, watching me all the while. "The last week and a half or so, I've been infiltrating an archaeological dig in Croatia, to prevent some ancient magical artefacts from falling into human hands. When I was there, I came across a collection of old documents. The head archaeologist said that most of them were just trade records, tallying the sale of produce and livestock, that sort of thing, or shipping manifests. He did get really excited about this."

Neja handed me the plastic and I took it, turning it over in my hands, but not looking at it. I was watching Neja, waiting for the punchline. This was what she wanted to talk to me about three days ago. This was the clue that she'd found regarding my soul. Now, with the strange, monstrous power writhing beneath my skin, I was even more interested to get my soul back, to get back at least some semblance of control over my life. What was left of it, that is.

Neja ran her hands over the leather of her jacket, watching me in return. She sighed. "He said it's a document that's maybe seven hundred years old. Maybe more. Maybe less. But the part that he was really interested in, Cal, is that it's written with a ball-point pen. In English. And I recognised the handwriting."

I finally read the paper, a tiny scrap that was frayed at the edges and likely made of some sort of animal skin. The ink was faded, but still even more precise than I had anticipated. It was small, hardly more than a scrap, but suddenly beyond significant. Way beyond.

I stared at the paper, falling apart and absolutely, completely, impossible. I looked up at Neja, my mouth open.

"This...it can't..." I couldn't breathe.

"Cal, I had it authenticated," Neja said, placing a hand on my arm. "It's real. Not some hoax, not some fake. It really was written in Croatia, some seven hundred years ago. It's real, Cal."

I looked down at the tiny scrap of paper that would surely disintegrate in my hands. It was a note. Hand-written. Only, the handwriting was mine.

My employment was a mistake.

- Cal Thorpe, Marketing Agent.

ACKNOWLEDGMENTS

I should, above everything else, like to thank my own crazy pets for the inspiration. Mischief and Mayhem wouldn't have come about if it weren't for my pup, Sammy. And Shakespeare got all of his grumpiness from Leah, the unquestionable Queen of the Universe. Minnie, the newest member of the family, gave all the energy.

Thank you also to my family, who support me even as I throw Cal into more unfortunate situations. I'm pretty sure they'd support me even if I threw Cal into fortunate situations, but I think I'll stick with the status quo. It's more entertaining that way. Sorry, Cal.

A special thanks to my cover designer, Fay Lane, whose work on all these books puts a smile on my face no matter how many times I see them. She takes my requests in stride, and I appreciate that a great deal.

And thank you to all my readers, who stick with me on these strange journeys.

ABOUT THE AUTHOR

E.G. Stone is an independent author who has been writing, creating and causing vast amounts of trouble since the age of six. Since then, E.G. has improved rather a lot in both the trouble-causing and writing and now spends her time writing fantasy and science fiction. When not writing, she is off musing about the workings of languages, both real and created, or drawing and sewing. E.G. reads voraciously, perhaps to the point of slight-insanity. Weird, nerdy, perhaps a little crazy, she is having a grand old time writing, reading, reviewing, interviewing, and, naturally, continuing her endeavours in causing trouble.

ALSO BY E. G. STONE

The Wing Cycle:

The One Who Could Not Fly

To Never Hear the Song

The Forsaking of the Blind

On Behalf of Death:

The Innocence of Death

Knowledge Aforethought

A Party of Certainties

When Death's Away

Mischief, Mayhem and Shakespeare

The Long Way Home

Other Titles:

The Crow and the King

Speaker of Words

Pestilence and Plague: An Anthology of Stories about the
Virus

9 781954 865037